The King's Raven

Ed Thilenius

Copyright 2018 Ed Thilenius

All rights reserved. No part of this publication may be reproduced, distributed, or transmitted in any form or by any means, including photocopying, recording, or other electronic or mechanical methods, without the prior written permission of the publisher, except in the case of brief quotations embodied in critical reviews and certain other noncommercial uses permitted by copyright law.

Printed in the United States of America

First Printing, 2018

ISBN-13: 978-0-692-16313-9

This book is primarily a work of fiction. Any references to historical events, real people, or real places are used fictitiously. Other names, characters, places and events are products of the author's imagination, and any resemblances to actual events or places or persons, living or dead, is entirely coincidental.

DEDICATION

This book is dedicated to my darling wife Debbie.

Thank you to all my family, friends, and fans of my first novel, *Wolf on the Lake*. Your faith in my books and your unending encouragement have made this second—and soon third—book possible.

Also, many thanks to the great people at Durham Editing and E-books. Your wisdom, advice, and being the best editing company in the world have made my books shine. Thank you for everything.

CONTENTS

Introduction	i
Chapter 1: Henry VIII and His Friend Caesar	1
Chapter 2: An Unholy Alliance	5
Chapter 3: A Secret Emerges	10
Chapter 4: A New Commission	14
Chapter 5: Recovery	18
Chapter 6: The Moment	22
Chapter 7: The Beginning of the Curse	24
Chapter 8: Pizza Night in England	26
Chapter 9: The Horn and the Hound Pub	29
Chapter 10: What Goes In, Must Come Out	34
Chapter 11: Corrections and New Orders	39
Chapter 12: Palace of Whitehall	43
Chapter 13: A Treacherous Night at the Inn	47
Chapter 14: Fish, Crabs, and Other Things	52
Chapter 15: If a Piece of Wood Could Talk	54
Chapter 16: Essex and Chelmsford Cathedral	60
Chapter 17: Hello, Evil, We Have Met Before	64
Chapter 18: The Back of the Bus Has the Best Seats	70
Chapter 19: After Him	73
Chapter 20: Knock… Knock?	75
Chapter 21: The Scent of Death	77
Chapter 22: A Wake-Up Call Won't Be Needed	79
Chapter 23: What Have They Done to Our King?	81
Chapter 24: Rush Hour	85
Chapter 25: A Mouse and a Mole	87
Chapter 26: Breaking News	89
Chapter 27: Remember to Serve	92
Chapter 28: A Wolf in the Room and Another at the Door	96
Chapter 29: Restart	98
Chapter 30: Evil Has a Shadow	100
Chapter 31: Let's Go to Church	101
Chapter 32: Terminating a File	103
Chapter 33: A Visit to the Undercroft	105
Chapter 34: What's in the Box?	108
Chapter 35: Protect, Save, Serve	112
Chapter 36: An Unholy Charge	114
Chapter 37: Cassandra's Ring	119

Chapter 38: The Raven Says Yes	120
Chapter 39: The Hunters Begin to Close In	123
Chapter 40: Trapped	126
Chapter 41: The Trap Is Sprung	130
Chapter 42: In the Shadow of the Crow	133
Chapter 43: A Dance with Death in the Air	137
Epilogue	140

INTRODUCTION

Devotion is love, loyalty, and zeal for a person, group, passion, or deity. Worship is adoration and reverence for a unique individual or deity. Loyalty is a strong feeling of allegiance or faithfulness. These three words have shaped history, as man has always had a sense of pride and passion for any leader he admires or even a deity adores. He believes in these ideals, for it is in his childhood that his need or desire for a leader is born.

Men need a father figure that they can look up to and claim as their own. They are often hopelessly locked in the belief that service to this father figure will bring approval and grace. It is also in this adoration that a unique trap lies. Like blinders on a draft animal, this devotion limits the individual to a sheer, one-sided belief. Any thought contrary to the devotion is foreign and considered an obstacle or even an enemy. Such feelings could not be better exemplified than by the vergers of King Henry VIII of England.

The verger during Henry VIII's time (1491-1547) wore a soldier's tunic, which designated him as a member of the House Guard, yet he bore no semblance at all to a regular castle garrison elite. He was special in another way: he was one of the king's unique soldiers, a verger (from the Latin word "*virga*," meaning staff or rod.). Created by His Majesty to protect clergy of all types, a verger's responsibility back then was to escort the Anglican brethren when outside the safety of a church or cathedral's walls and protect them from vandals or, even worse, the beggars asking for alms for the poor when their sole intent was to keep the money.

These men were hired from the ranks of the English army. Usually, they were recruited from the lower ranks or other militia who were not dutifully employed by a knight or a lord. These soldiers were armed only with simple weapons, like a staff, mace, or even a spear. They rarely carried a sword, and most of these loyal guards carried no armor. They were, though, specially regarded as necessary for the clergy's protection as England's new religion began to take shape through the throws of being an excommunicated kingdom from the Roman Catholic Church.

Henry had wanted a divorce from his wife Catherine, since the young queen could bear him no male heir. His Highness asked the Pope in Rome for an annulment, only to be told that the Holy Father Pope Clement VII would need time to think about this request. Catherine's brother King Charles V, commander of the Holy Roman Empire, with his armies, got wind of this request. Dreading the embarrassment and disgrace of a divorce by his sister, King Charles sent a message via envoy to the Pope in Rome saying, "Grant Henry's request for a divorce from my sister, and I will launch my armies on Rome and sack the city and you with it!"

Quickly, the Pope changed his vacillations, and His Eminence sent word to Henry in England that no divorce request would be granted.

Henry VIII, noble king and defender of the Roman Catholic faith, many times awarded by the Pope for his undying loyalty to Rome, was furious and had had enough. He wanted an heir to his kingdom, and he would have one. Pope's blessing or not, he would have his way.

At that point, he was approached by his archbishop, Thomas Cranmer. Cranmer advised his king that since he was of noble birth and blood and appointed by God already, that the blessings of Rome were not needed. As long as there was an heir to succeed his lineage, no Roman Catholic acknowledgement to the crown would be needed. Besides, Henry was God's "righthand man," so said the Catholic Church, so who was to say he couldn't form his own church, a church that represented English viewpoints for God Himself to sort? This began the great break from the church, and a new religion was formed, the Anglican Church, or Church of the English.

When Henry VIII died, his body was buried in a vault without a formal tomb. He shared that vault in Windsor Castle with his only wife who bore him a legitimate heir, Jane Seymore; the beheaded King Charles I; and an infant child of Queen Anne. In 1837, some three hundred years after Henry's death, King William IV ordered a formal marker to be placed in St. George's Chapel, which is inside Windsor Castle. This marker, a black marble slab, is in the center of a black and white harlequin floor. Black as a raven's wing, the marker shows all who reads it that King Henry VIII's deposited remains rest in peace there. It is, indeed, a much-revered place for any verger who comes to pay homage, as I have done.

As author of this book, I will intrigue you with a plot that will uncover a secret known only by a select few: that Henry VIII's body went missing for several days before he was placed in that burial vault. Believed to have been stolen, a desperate search was made until His Majesty's body could be recovered and the perpetrators dealt with.

I was a verger for the Episcopal Church for 12 years in the United States. I have participated in pilgrimages to Europe and have served as a layperson in Anglican services at Canterbury and Walsingham, England, two of our most revered places in Anglican worship. I have seen only a few of the sacred, yet secret, locations for the vergers in England, France, the United States, and even Rome, Italy. Other shrines and vaults contain the many secrets known only to certified vergers or porters, who are actual members of a select few within the Verger's Guild.

The standard symbol for a verger is the crossed keys or crossed maces. The guild I will be referring to will have the monstrance marked with the letters "GDO," or *"Guilde des Os,"* as its own symbol. This represents the secret order of vergers who protect Henry VIII's relics. (Look for antique gold, silver, or bronze monstrance lapel pins which denote their rank within their order to find them.) I wear one on special trips to Europe.

Not even the priests or rectors are privy to a verger's knowledge of King Henry VIII's bones, for their journeys take them to many parishes. This prohibits them from protecting what is so treasured and secret. The artifacts and places mentioned in this book do exist, and it is my duty to tell their story to help me protect these locations from an ancient foe bent on changing history to their needs.

This is not a betraying of the guild, for I have been a loyal and devoted verger. This is merely a plea to the reader to help us find a lost treasure, a treasure that is very dear to the church and to the guild at large. This story is of a feud between two factions from two countries, two religious beliefs, and a secret battle that still exists to this day. This war is vehemently denied by both sides for much is at stake.

CHAPTER 1: HENRY VIII AND HIS FRIEND CAESAR

France, 1513

The battlefield was cold with a heavy dark gray overcast that morning. A lone black raven circled overhead to choose a convenient place to perch and watch. Surveying the many humans standing in strange rows and groups on the open field, the raven widened its circular pattern to expand its search for a resting place. The humans on one side of the field spoke the language of that land. Those men seemed restless to the gliding bird. One of their archers shot an arrow at the raven, but it missed and flew past him.

The raven's circle took it across to the other side of the battlefield. There the men wore red clothing and hats that looked like salad bowls. A royal entourage of the red-clothed humans assembled on a small knoll. One human, his master, wore resplendent metal clothing and looked very impressive standing before the camp's large banner. The black bird swooped down and landed on a golden lion on top of the stick which held the banner. The black raven cawed four caws to say it was happy. The great leader looked up at his raven and let out a hardy laugh.

"Thank you, my good sir," he said to the bird. "Cheer up, men! We have Caesar on our side!"

The royal staff let out a sigh of relief and joined their king's laughter.

King Henry VIII's army was in France for his third war on the continent of Europe, and he hoped it would be his last. The pivotal battle before him would finalize his claim that he was the rightful king of Normandy. Sadly, the French defenders were not going to lay down their arms so easily. Frenchmen, Normans, Swiss mercenaries, and even members of the Holy Roman Empire were assembled to oppose the

English king. Across the battlefield from Henry's army stood these amassed forces.

Of the hundreds of crossbow men, men-at-arms, and knights, both mounted and on foot, assembled to defeat Henry's army, one battle unit was made of entirely of mounted knights. They were known as the Knights of the Cuirassier. These large men on horses wore polished armor and looked extremely professional in front of their blue banner with its white flower. They made no sound. There was no talking, and even their horses were eerily silent.

The wind picked up, announcing an approaching storm with heavy black clouds.

"Looks like foul weather, my liege," said one of the Cuirassier Knights to their leader. "We will need to finish this battle soon before the rains mire our horses in the mud."

"Like at Agincourt," said another.

"Enough," commanded the leader, raising his hand to silence his men. "Raise the black flag."

Back on the other side of the battlefield, gathered in a group, stood King Henry, his entourage of advisors, and the members of his court. The black raven perched on the king's banner flapped its wings as if alerting Henry's men of some impending dread. Caesar let out three caws in quick succession, meaning danger.

"Sire, your friend has noticed something," cautioned an advisor as he pointed across the battlefield. "The French have raised the black flag, Your Grace, which means no surrender, no quarter, and no prisoners."

Henry looked up at the raven and tipped his bonnet in thanks to his feathered friend. He turned back to his advisors and smiled.

"Well, if those pretty French knights want to play rough, then so shall we," Henry announced with a stern look. He slammed his fist into the palm of his other hand. "No quarter to that group. If any mercenary or Holy Roman soldier wishes to surrender or yields, honor it. We will need new troops to fight again if necessary. But those impudent bastards who wave the black flag… tear them up! The order is given. Grind their bones! Tell my army to grind their bones!"

The raven let out another three caws. Then Caesar flew to a wooden table that was being used to display a map of the battlefield. There was an ink well holding down one of the corners of the map. The large raven tipped over the feathered quill and caused the ink well to spill onto the map.

An advisor cursed loudly at the king's pet causing His Majesty and the others to turn around to see what the commotion was about. The raven with his large leathered claws then proceeded to walk into the black liquid. Next, he proceeded to walk to a clear part on the parchment, and as he walked, the pitchfork-like markings of his footprints slowly and magically changed shape. The scratches then became words. What was once black ink marks had morphed into the words "NO SIRE."

Henry walked over to the table, his eyes narrowing as he gazed at the markings. "'No sire'? What the devil is our little friend trying to write?"

The others surrounding Henry backed away with fear in their eyes.

"'Tis witchcraft and devilry, Your Grace," whispered one of the stewards. "Foul tidings from Rome after we broke away from the Vatican."

"Shall I kill this abomination, Your Majesty?" asked another as he drew his sword four inches from the scabbard and stared at the black bird warily.

"Touch him and your King will die!" came a cackled old voice from the bottom of the grassy knoll.

No one had noticed the old crone in her tattered gray rags and shawl until that moment. Appearing out of the mists, she didn't seem real, yet everyone, including the king, heard her voice.

The steward finished unsheathing his sword and cried, "Kill her!"

"Hold!" the King said, raising his arm. He tilted his head slightly and then placed both hands on the table, leaning onto his mighty arms. "Let her speak."

The old woman slowly climbed the hill as the men moved in closer to Henry. His faithful steward had sheathed his sword, but his hand did not leave it. Henry waited patiently, eyeing the woman as she moved towards them like a wraith sliding through the mist.

"You know who I am, my lord," the old woman said as she reached the top of the knoll and stopped. "We have met before when you were much younger. I was the keeper of the lost art and the religion your monks abandoned when you worshipped the new Christian faith. Your ancestors used to call on me whenever they were unsure of things."

Henry searched the woman's face, struggling to place her. He leaned further onto his arms, stretching himself closer to get a better look. A look of recognition swept across his face, and his eyes widened.

A haggard smile crept across the woman's face. "This battle today, you will win. The French army will be quickly defeated, and the mercenaries will flee once they know there is no more money to pay them."

Henry nodded, but before he could speak, the woman continued.

"It is the knights with the blue banner and white flower that you must be careful of." She moved in close to the table and whispered, "These are not ordinary men. They worship a darker evil—that I know. Yet I cannot see through it. They are not Christian, and they use that flag to make them less conspicuous. They will haunt your steps, sire. Defeat the other armies, but, sire, give those dark knights a wide berth. They are your doom."

The king's entourage stood silent. No one uttered a word. The sound of the winds picked up as the trees in the nearby wood swayed in the air.

Henry straightened himself and nodded. "I fear no man, crone, but I feared you the first time we met ages ago."

The witch bowed quietly with respect. Henry's raven friend flew off the table and landed on the crone's walking staff and cawed four times indicating he was happy. Henry looked at Caesar and took a deep breath.

"Very well," Henry said as he nodded to the old woman. "You shall remain on my staff for council. Stay back and out of the way. What should my men call you?"

The witch reached out and stroked Caesar's head, her wrinkled fingers running up and down his sleek black feathers. "You have always known me as Cassandra, warden of the ravens and crows who are my subjects. They can be a great ally, my king."

"I can use all the allies I can muster," laughed the king as he looked out across the battlefield.

In the distance, on the French side, war drums could be heard signaling the advance. A horn sounded for the French cavalry to push forward.

CHAPTER 2: AN UNHOLY ALLIANCE

France, 1513

King Henry gazed at the advance and was alarmed at the speed of the mounted Cuirassier knights across the field of battle. The mounted knights beneath their blue banner with its white flower didn't have horns blaring or drums pounding. The silence of their movement brought out the caution in Henry. Indeed, it was a terrible sight to behold. The foreboding knights trotting in a silent line abreast led the entire French force forward.

Henry realized the very soldiers he was to avoid fighting were, indeed, the very first ones he would encounter. He also knew if he gave up the fight at that point, his retreating army would be broken in morale and ruthlessly cut down like wheat before a scythe. His advisors and the members of his royal court stood behind him, anxiously awaiting his orders.

Henry looked at Cassandra for an answer to this riddle. Her head was bowed as if in a trance. Her staff was held by both hands, tapping the ground below as if she was summoning something from the earth beneath her. Caesar flew off her staff only to rest on another banner pole.

Henry looked out across the field once more and then slammed his fist on the table before him. "If only the mercenaries and allies to the French attack were not there, the dark knights would be outnumbered and would surely leave, giving us control of this land."

"As you wish, my lord," spoke the crone's voice inside Henry's head, and he spun around to look at her. Her head was still bowed, and she continued to strike the ground with her staff.

Again, her voice spoke within Henry's mind. "But first, I must have payment to complete this task. Bring my ways of the forest and the druids back. Give me and my followers protection from your religious zealots and leave us in peace. In return, I will give you your victory."

Henry held his hand to his head as anger surged through him. Unsure if he was going mad, he hesitated to answer her out loud. The anger over her treachery was too great, and he said out loud, "You dare to blackmail your king?"

Henry's men looked at each other in shock and dismay, unsure of what Henry was talking about. They wondered if the witch had placed him under some spell and slowly began to back away from him for fear of being placed under her spell themselves.

"You do not have an answer to this riddle before you, my king," the crone's voice replied in his mind.

Henry shook his head, holding it in both hands to pry the words from his mind. He turned back to the battlefield. The Cuirassier knights inched closer and closer, and he knew he was helpless. He rested his arms on the table and bowed his head. In a haggard voice, he said, "Very well, Cassandra. You have your wish."

The crone's voice resounded in his mind again. "Swear it."

"I gave you my word, crone," Henry hissed as his men backed further away from him. "Now do it."

Again, the words rang out in his mind. "Swear it."

Henry spun around and pounded his fist on the breastplate of his armor. "All right, you infernal hag! I swear it!"

Cassandra's staff stopped moving, and she looked up at him, her eyes glassy and black. Henry stepped backwards, and several of his advisors turned and ran. His faithful steward unsheathed his sword and took a step towards the witch, but Henry threw his arm out and blocked his path.

"It is done," she said.

In an instant, four large ravens dropped from the sky. Their black forms were amazingly swift in the air as each flew into the ranks of the mercenaries made of Swiss legions and Holy Roman Army soldiers. Each of the large birds dropped a rolled piece of parchment tied with a gray ribbon of cloth that seemed to be cut from Cassandra's clothing. Each scroll was written in the language of the recipient, and each was written in the crow's style, using their feet and ink.

The notes all said the same thing: "There is no gold left. You will all die here with no one to bury you. Your army is fighting a lost cause."

With the messages delivered, small to large groups of men huddled together to read or hear what the messages said. The masses looked like ants drawn to a sugar drop. Each group of men stayed as one, and then, just as quick, broke apart and dissipated into the woods, fields, and roads. The massive French host slowly broke ranks and cohesiveness as their allies' soldiers lost heart and turned around to flee homeward. The mercenaries began to leave en masse, and only a handful of men with pikes and a few militia units remained behind the dark knights.

In amazement, Henry's advisors and stewards slowly moved forward and gathered beside Henry at the table to look out across the battlefield. They couldn't believe their luck. The huge army was vanishing before their eyes, and they felt sure that the feared dark horsemen with their blue banner and black flag would turn and run.

Henry was pleased and looked back at Cassandra with a smile, feeling that, perhaps, the bargain could be kept. France was a big place, and he could possibly allow her religion to thrive there instead of back home. He had to think on that possibility carefully because he knew that dealing with crones and witches could be one's undoing. Still, Henry was pleased that he would win the battle that day as he turned to look back over the battlefield.

At that moment, something changed. The clouds split open as Henry's men began to charge without orders, racing headlong into the remnants of the mercenaries and the knights upfront. Henry turned to look at Cassandra, whose face was dark surrounding her glassy, dark eyes. Confusion spread through the leaders quickly, and Henry knew they had to do something as the thought of Cassandra's warning resounded in his mind.

"To your horses!" Henry commanded. "We must take control of our forces!"

Knowing of the witch's foreboding tale of doom, the leaders mounted their horses as Henry clamored to mount his horse in his heavy armor. He looked over, but the crone had vanished as if melted by the pouring rain. The leaders took off down the hill through the pouring rain towards the charging men. Henry took one last look around the hilltop searching for Cassandra before he charged forward to try to take control of the charge that had already begun.

The Cuirassier knights across the field, realizing that they have been abandoned by most of the army, broke from their silence and shouted protests to retire to their leaders. The head of the column continued the charge, the black flag imitating the raging storm clouds above their heads as the attack continued. A few of the knights turned to retreat and were faced with the remaining English macemen and pikes charging pell-mell towards them. The cowardly were quickly slaughtered by the back ranks: no one was to disobey.

The massive body of men and horses on the French side quickly began to tire in the soft field as the charge turned into a gallop. The large horses frothed in thirst as they labored to carry their masters up the gentle rise towards the oncoming English.

Henry's leaders tried vainly to recall their men as they charged to the front of the attack as Henry himself raced forward.

"No, men! My soldiers, stay! Hold! Stop!" he yelled.

The other commanders followed suit, but to no avail. The army smelled blood and wanted those riches. Gilded armor, priceless weapons of the elite, and the large war horses were too much of a siren's call to the peasant soldiers. A great sword made by the finest Italian armorers could bring several years' wages and food to an ordinary man's family. The charge of the English forces was an unstoppable juggernaut of men and horse. Like a man dying of thirst and seeing an oasis just yards away, the English soldiers wanted those riches.

Cassandra entered Henry's mind once again. "Stop them now, or your curse will haunt your bones for eternity."

Hearing the crone's voice in his head, Henry spurred his warhorse ever forward. He desperately wanted his men to stop. The men, however, mistook their king's charging as encouragement and thought the king wanted some of the riches as well. This sparked a frantic race towards the enemy.

When the armies clashed, it was like a clap of thunder. Some of the Frenchmen's horses were slaughtered upon the English pikes, and in return, the Cuirassier knights crushed the charging English militia.

To a bystander standing on a distant hilltop looking at the battle below, the French nobility on horses looked like one massive steel elephant of great strength. Each thrust, each slash and deadly swing, looked like a massive beast with great tusks that was slicing, stomping, and crushing its attacker.

The English forces, in return, were like a horde of army ants devouring the mighty elephant in pieces. The Cuirassier knights with their black flag were butchered. The blue and white banner lay in tatters, covered in mud. No French soldier dared to pick up the standards, for they feared instant reprisal in doing so. A few of the king's advisors, however, collected pieces the banner as trophies of war.

"The king said to grind their bones! Come on, boys! Let's have some fun! Let's grind them!" yelled a grizzled English swordsman with only three teeth left in his mouth damaged from decay.

The English soldiers ravaged the remaining French and their allies. It took only minutes, but the dark knights were destroyed. Every knight was dismounted and dismembered. Their suits of plate armor, the finest in the land made by Italian master smiths, only weighed down the trapped Frenchmen as English soldiers with small knives and picks broke and stabbed their way through the armor's slits and openings. Some of the French knights tried to surrender, but since they had flown the black flag to begin with, no one had pity on them that their plans fell flat. They were killed as well.

A lone French knight was being broken open by an inexperienced English mercenary. The French knight was wounded and spoke in English to the soldier, telling him that if he helped him out his armored suit, he would show the Englishman where his silver coins were hidden. The naïve soldier obliged and, once all the armor was removed, helped to sit the French knight up and waited for the French nobleman to give him his loot. The English soldier never saw the steel gauntlet that the knight still had on as it bashed his skull in.

In the mud amidst the gruesome scene, the frantic knight put on the dead man's tunic and scampered away to the nearby wood. When challenged by another English soldier where was he going, the French knight, in his best English accent, said he had the runs and didn't want to soil his clothing.

Henry stopped his horse and slowly exhaled as he surveyed the carnage before him. He was too late. The massacre was complete. He bowed his head and whispered, "Cassandra's curse will come true."

CHAPTER 3: A SECRET EMERGES

Afghanistan, 2014

The Afghan night was cold and dusty. The dark sky was almost a purple black with the moon barely visible in a crescent shrouded by cirrus clouds of ice. To the left side of the valley, the British garrisoned outpost was settling down for the evening. Lookouts and sentries for the British forces were in the process of changing shifts.

This outpost was an advance base designed for artillery support with a battery of L118 105mm light guns, manned by the 93rd Le Cateau battery of the 5th Regiment of the Royal Artillery. These men and women were the proud members of this very distinguished unit of the British army whose decisive stand was near the tiny village of Le Cateau, France, during the First World War.

For the unit in Afghanistan, their guns' primary duty was to protect the airfield that was west of the firebase. There was also a village within the fire support sectors that needed constant protection and support.

That cold night, it was truer than ever. Just outside the village, on a road that led to the British base, was an important supply and communication path. It allowed rapid response units to exit the outpost, and it also allowed mobile combat units to hunt down and destroy any known approaching threat. The British army excelled in that tactic and often likened it to when the United States' cavalry came to the rescue of besieged settlers during the American Indian wars.

Two militants had carefully timed the moon phase when it would be very dark yet light enough to see to walk and work in. They also knew the time when the British troops had a shift change. These two shadowy figures worked quietly as they dug a hole underneath the road's path to lay an Improvised Explosive Device, or IED.

The thinner militant tossed his spade aside as he crouched next to his partner who was already working on the device. The lean, dark-skinned man looked cautiously up and down the road. "Careful, my brother. We don't want to make any mistake with the connecting of the arming device. The cellphone detonator is ready to go."

"The artillery shell is heavy, and I've carried this damn thing all day. Don't tell me to be careful. I'm just glad to get rid of it," the larger man said vehemently as a smile spread across his face. "This will kill many English soldiers tomorrow."

The men finished connecting the two detonator wires and began placing dirt and rocks back over the bomb. For added realism, they pulled the carcass of a dead dog over the fresh dirt mound. As an additional trick, the taller terrorist attached a pair of English identification tags to the dog's neck. Valued and worn by every soldier, ID tags were the only way a deceased soldier's remains could be identified. If anything, this cunning addition to their ploy would make a soldier come closer to inspect.

The operation was complete, and the two men quietly collected their digging tools. They had not yet begun to move away when above them, just on the other side of a sand berm, arose an American Army drone. It was four feet wide and had six propellers. It carried the menacing name "Wolf." Beneath the craft was a camera and a large cone antennae.

The vehicle swooped in and surprised the two intruders. The six rotary motors humming in unison sounded like a small swarm of angry bees which alarmed the militants that their bomb surprise had been discovered. The drone made a single pass just over the heads of the enemy and flew a safe distance to the other side of the road.

At the British outpost, American Army officer Lt. Michael Cotter of Georgia skimmed his tanned hand over his short, dark brown hair as he watched the drone's feed. He glanced quickly over his shoulder towards the dignified man who stood across the room looking at another monitor. "I've got two intruders who just got caught red-handed, Captain Mons."

Captain Mons, whose great-great-grandfather had been an artillery officer for the Royal Artillery during the early stages of the First World War, quietly approached the American attaché to observe his findings. Lt. Cotter, who had joined the Army right after college, was on loan from his combat unit, the 10th Mountain, to help support British Army operations in drone technology. The years as an ROTC cadet in college had paid off for Michael, as he had gone straight into Officer Candidate School and had specialized in surveillance and advanced drone technology. Electronics had been his hobby since high school when he, his brother Steve, and their cousin Elizabeth had built a homemade submarine called Wolf and enjoyed the beautiful summer on Lake Lanier. Four years had passed since that time on the lake.

The 5th Regiment where Lt. Cotter was currently stationed was part of the Surveillance and Target Acquisition Section, and drones were the new way to conduct military warfare. He had been assigned to that posting to support the firebase and provide perimeter security. Michael had finally been recognized for his talents in that posting and was helping his country, and the world, while doing what he loved

Michael's new Wolf, the drone, was not armed with combat weapons, but it did carry a nighttime camera and a daytime camera, as well as a special bit of technology on loan from the Israeli Army. The Shiska ATD sensor was the latest instrument capable of detecting an IED device using any form of telecommunication as a detonator. The Israelis used their Shiskas on every vehicle that had to travel through hostile territory. The device broadcasted a radio frequency on every band to detonate any device attached to a cellphone that was waiting for an activating phone call. The success rate in finding those IEDs was ninety-two percent. Many soldiers were willing to accept those odds.

The British captain stroked his sleek mustache as he leaned over Michael to analyze the video feed of the two suspects. Observing the signal strength of the threat meter coming from the Shiska, Captain Mons was convinced the men were a viable target.

"Give our guests a ring," smirked the captain as he stood and straightened the front of his brown and green camouflage shirt with its red piping and red tabs on the collar.

Michael quickly hit the activation switch, which sent a feedback loop radio wave from the small dome underneath the drone's fuselage. This signal infiltrated its way back through the cellphone held by one of the bombers whose phone number was connected to the warhead buried under the road. The signal peaked at the highest signal strength which detonated the explosive. The terrorists own bomb exploded with such ferocity that it instantly vaporized the two enemy militants. The shockwave from the blast caused Michael's drone to rock backwards before the gyro stabilizers kicked in to right the craft.

Captain Mons patted Michael on the back. The captain, known for being all red tabs and *bon ami*, couldn't help but smile down at the young American for the success of the drone's interception. One by one, everyone in the surveillance hut congratulated Michael with pats on his back. Cheers to the American and Israeli technology filled the room.

As the others continued in their celebration, Michael turned the drone around and made a lower, slower pass over the detonation area. The blast had been a big one and would have killed many soldiers or civilians who used the road to do their daily tasks. No remnants of the two men were visible, except for one lonely black tennis shoe still smoking from the explosion.

Michael continued to fly the Wolf in a broad circular path to survey the base's perimeter. He kept the drone at an altitude of 200 feet as it made its way around the village and proceeded to the other side of the base.

A series of small dunes formed an excellent backdrop for the British soldiers to conduct firing practice, but the dunes made it difficult to have a secure 360-degree perimeter. Michael slowed the Wolf to almost a standstill to allow the Shiska to scan this new area. He looked at the meter readings which showed inconclusive results. He remembered when he had been briefed by the Israelis that the Shiska did not perform well at higher altitudes due to normal cellphone traffic and radio frequencies. He glanced again at the night camera and saw no odd shapes in the dunes or nearby areas. He did notice an old wadi that snaked its way along a dry river bed. He dove the Wolf into the wadi and followed the path to the river bed.

What he then saw startled him. Michael's Wolf discovered at least 150 militants armed with RPGs and automatic weapons. The Shiska meter sounded an alarm meaning energy spikes.

"Oh, shit!" Michael gasped as his Wolf had just stumbled across an assembly area where the ISIS militants had assembled and were preparing to attack.

"Captain Mons!" he shouted, his brown eyes glued to the screen before him.

The other soldiers in the hut stopped their celebrations and turned to see Michael's discovery. All eyes were on the visual monitor.

The Wolf started rocking back and forth. Michael tried to compensate by moving the drone to the left and right, but something was disturbing the flight path of the drone.

Outside, gunfire could be heard followed by mortars firing in the distance. The base was under attack. The unusual rocking was actually from bullets attempting to shoot down the drone. The Wolf was taking fire.

"Stand to!" commanded the captain.

The entire base went into action. Explosions rocked the camp as soldiers scrambled to their gun positions. Others manned machine gun emplacements and returned fire as RPG rockets crisscrossed the night sky like a dazzling firework show, only the rockets were meant to kill not to entertain.

CHAPTER 4: A NEW COMMISSION

Afghanistan, 2014

Everyone left the hut once the attack started except for Michael and his sandy-haired English friend, Lance Corporal David B. Brown. Both men were well-respected for their talents in drone surveillance and base security, and it didn't surprise Michael that they would be the two left in charge of trying to use the drones to take out any possible detonation devices that the militants still had on them.

David and Michael had hit it off instantly as friends, despite such a friendship being regarded as taboo between officers and enlisted men. David had taken the time to talk with Michael about the ways of the British Army, its traditions and quirks. David, a member of the Church of England, had listened respectfully while Michael had talked about his Episcopal church back in Gainesville, Georgia. Both men had shared their love for their churches and had often joked about the American Revolution and how it had messed things up for them to have been from the same church. Michael had served as a verger in his home church, and it had really sealed their friendship when David had revealed that he, too, served as a porter, or verger, at his church, the Cathedral at Chelmsford, Essex, in England. From time to time, David had worn a very nice golden ring with a verger symbol on it. When asked about it, David had always shrugged it off, saying it had been a small token of respect for serving as a verger. Michael had always wondered why he hadn't gotten such a ring back in the States.

Michael glanced over his shoulder at his friend who was working intently at the screen before him then turned back to monitor the Wolf. He was certainly thankful for the friendship that he and David had developed. While the others they were stationed with spent their free time partying or drinking, Michael and David preferred a quieter existence. They spent their free time playing chess or talking about their hobbies or their churches. For some reason, sitting there in the midst of the attack, Michael found himself thinking of David's church.

He had known of David's church but had not visited it when he and his family had gone on vacation to the United Kingdom. The closest Michael had gotten to any Anglican church had been Canterbury Cathedral. It had been in early June, and he'd had too much coffee for breakfast. He had wandered off from his family's tour group to a collection of buildings to the side of the cathedral. He'd spotted the men's room and proceeded in to relieve himself. While there, he had heard there was a group from Texas that was visiting there as well that day.

Curious, after he finished in the men's room, Michael had wandered over to the side entrance of the Cathedral and had gone inside. The magnificent cathedral had been beyond description. Immense columns, grandiose architecture, and the staff had all combined into a great work of art.

"Are you with the group from Texas?" an aging verger had asked.

Startled, Michael had jumped slightly before turning to look at the grey-haired man beside him. "No. I am from Georgia. I am a verger from America with a group of Episcopalians from our church in Gainesville, Georgia, and others from our cathedral in Atlanta, the Cathedral of St. Philip."

"St. Philip in Atlanta? Oh, yes, you are most welcome." The verger had smiled broadly as he pointed towards a set of pews to the right side of the church. "We have some extra seats. Take that row behind the Texans. You do get along with these people, yes?"

Michael had chuckled. "Oh, yes, sir. We have been brothers ever since our civil war."

"Oh, that, yes," the verger had replied, his round face flushing a bit. "We had our own civil war, Royalists and Roundheads. Off with his head and all that nonsense. War is terrible, don't you think?"

"Yes, sir, most terrible. Thank goodness there is peace."

A few minutes later, Michael's church group had then walked through the main entrance only to find Michael grinning from ear to ear. He had been sitting midway through the church with aisle seating, and they had suddenly realized they had a priority row during that particular church's service. Many had praised Michael for his ingenuity. It had been a happy time for Michael then.

Michael blinked himself out of his daydream and focused back on the battle. He maneuvered the Wolf to recover from the shots being fired at it, and he brought the drone around to assist the camp in defending itself. The big artillery guns began a series of rapid short-range attacks which decimated the reverse ground the militants were hiding in. The barbed wire and anti-personnel mines thinned out the ranks of the enemy as well.

Michael sent another detonate command to the Shiska device on the Wolf. A number of explosions could be heard in the distance as three militants with suicide vests on were caught by the signal which detonated their vests. A total of fourteen assailants were killed by their own bombs.

Still, some enemy rounds found their marks. The cantina where the regiment enjoyed their meals took a direct hit. Fortunately, nobody was inside, but the breakfast materials being laid out for the morning were ruined. Michael knew when he saw the blasted structure from the drone's camera that the men would be disappointed since that morning's fair had included a unique delivery of blood sausage from the region of England where the regiment was from.

Another enemy mortar round successfully detonated a small ammunition cache. Bullets and grenade fragments exploded within the sandbagged bunker. In response, the British artillery and machine guns decimated the attackers. The few militant survivors retreated back into the wadi and escaped the base's wrath. A C-130 Hercules gunship had been called in to assist the British base with fire support. The ISIS fighters glowed white in the night-vision sensors equipped on the four-engine gunship. The plane's side-mounted Gatling machine gun ripped through the night air with the sound of a thousand rounds impacting the running targets some 200 meters down the wadi away from the base. None survived the air attack.

As the plane was pulling away, Michael brought the drone in due to a low battery light which signaled the end of the flight for the Wolf. Michael swung the craft in a perfect return flight and landed it on a damaged concrete pad next to the hut. Smiling, he turned to see David's reaction as to the near-perfect landing.

David didn't move. He was slumped over at his monitor with his head on the console. Blood had begun dripping to the floor, and Michael heard a wheezing sound coming from his chest. David had been hit by shrapnel.

Michael jumped up quickly and hurried to David's limp body. He helped his friend to sit upright. David was in a lot of pain as he held his head up; his lightly freckled face was pallid. The wound was to his chest and abdomen, and his brown and green camouflage uniform was soaked in red.

Weakly, David whispered, "Michael, I'm hit bad. Put me down on the floor. It hurts to sit up."

Michael carefully eased David to the floor and crouched down beside him. Michael cried out for a medic to come to the hut. He shouted loudly several times but wasn't heard past the last remaining sounds of battle outside.

David, realizing that he was in very bad shape, looked deeply into Michael's eyes as if searching for a sign or spark of assurance that he could trust Michael. He reached out and touched Michael's arm, drawing his attention from the door he had been watching in hopes of a medic.

"Michael, I've got to tell you something."

Michael looked back to the door and then down at his friend. "Hush, David. Save your strength, I've got to go and get the medics. You will only be alone for a minute."

David held on to Michael's sleeve with the last of his strength. "No, Michael, no. They won't make it in time, but you have got to listen to me."

Michael moved David's head closer to hear him and nodded.

"In my spare set of boots placed behind my footlocker, I hid a small wooden box wrapped in my underthings. You have to get that box back to England," David whispered in a haggard voice. He raised his free hand to his mouth as he coughed, and drops of blood covered the pale skin of his hand.

Michael searched his pockets and found a handkerchief. He pulled it out and placed it in David's hand.

"Go to the Cathedral in Chelmsford, England, and find the head verger named Lark. Give the box to him and tell him I'm sorry I took it. I had hoped... hoped...." David's words were cut off as he coughed heavily, blood spewing from his mouth.

Michael shook his head slightly, unsure of what to make of the mission his friend was asking him to undertake.

David coughed again and then continued. "I hoped it would save me from harm. I was wrong to take it. It is an ancient relic, and only he knows what it means. Trust no one else, Michael. Remember... to serve... to serve."

David coughed again and groaned in pain. His hand slowly let go of Michael's shirt. Michael lifted his friend's torso into his arms. Michael held David closely as the last breath left David's body.

The combat medic opened the door moments later, only to find Michael still cradling his dead friend. Covered in blood, Michael let out a deep sigh of pain and loss. The medic moved quickly across the room and dropped down beside the two men. He placed his fingers against David's neck to check for a pulse.

"He's gone," said the medic as he removed his fingers from David's neck.

Michael looked at the medic. He felt tired, and his vision blurred. Soon the medic's face was just a fuzzy image and then darkness. Michael collapsed on top of his dead friend from exhaustion and shock: he had been grazed in the neck by a piece of shrapnel and hadn't even known it.

CHAPTER 5: RECOVERY

Afghanistan, 2014

The next morning, Michael awoke with a headache and found a bandage around the right side of his neck. He touched the bandage and was instantly rewarded with a sharp pain.

"Damn!" he cried.

"Easy there, sir," responded an attendant who was standing next to the bed Michael was in.

Michael looked towards the man and then around the room. He realized he was in the recovery room of the infirmary.

"You got hit in the neck by some flying debris from a nearby blast," the attendant continued as he moved around the room working. "You're very lucky it didn't nick an artery, or you would have bled out and we would have one dead Yank on our hands."

"It hurts really bad," Michael responded with his hand cupped over the side of his neck.

"Right, we didn't want to give you a sedative or muscle relaxer until we knew you were going to come around. You had passed out on your friend David." The attendant stopped at the side of the bed and looked down before looking up at Michael. "I'm sorry for the loss of your mate."

Michael adjusted his position in bed and sat up. He looked over to the small desk next to his hospital bed and picked up a small glass of water. The English doctor overseeing Michael's condition had already prescribed some medication to ease the pain, and the bottle was on the far side of the desk. The orderly opened the bottle and gave a pill to Michael to swallow. Michael did so and put the glass back down.

"You should be feeling better in a little bit. Best you stay here until you know how strong that pill might be on you. It makes some lads sleepy and some dizzy. We'll see how it affects you. Do try to get some rest. You'll be shipping back to England with the rest of the wounded and the dead in the morning," said the orderly as he left the room. "England?" Michael closed his eyes and leaned back against the pillow. He thought about his friend dying in his arms. David had been the one person that he had related to while stationed at the base, but he was gone. The shock of it all had not set in. David's last words echoed through Michael's mind. He had made a promise to David and felt that it was his duty to see it to the end.

"I've got to get to David's locker to get that box he told me about," Michael said to himself as he slipped out from under the covers and put his feet into his infirmary slippers on the floor. He also put on a simple blue and white striped robe which covered his pajamas.

Michael shuffled across the floor to the door of the room. As he stepped outside, he was quickly blinded temporarily by the midday sun. He looked around at the damage that the British base had received during the previous night's raid. He then proceeded across the compound.

"Excuse me. Who are you, and what are you doing out of the infirmary?" asked a sergeant as he approached Michael from the flank.

"I'm Lieutenant Michael Cotter, U.S. Army, on assignment with your base," Michael responded as he came to a stop.

"Beg your pardon, Lt. Cotter, you being in your robe and all," the sergeant replied and then saluted with his palm facing outward.

Michael returned the salute.

"The attack has us all in a daze," the sergeant continued. "Be careful as you proceed to the old barracks. It caught fire during the attack, and a few of the bunks were destroyed with all the gear."

Michael nodded, and the sergeant again saluted him. Michael quickly returned the salute and crossed the parade ground. He then proceeded to the barracks and entered the dimly lit room.

The stench of burnt canvas, leather, nylon, and wood attacked his nostrils with an acid-like pungent smell as he looked around. There was only a single lightbulb still working on the other end of the room, which made his search for David's locker even harder. He gingerly stepped through the charred remains of several bunks and footlockers. He didn't see David's bunk. Michael began to panic as David's footlocker was nowhere to be found. The bed that David had slept in was burnt to a crisp. Beside the bed were only ashes and charred scraps.

Sadness began to creep into Michael's soul as his friend's dying request was vanishing like the smoke in the damaged bunkhouse.

"Can I help you?" asked a soldier with an unusual accent.

Michael turned to look at the man. The stocky, black-haired soldier wore the same brown and green camouflage clothes with red piping on them that the other British soldiers did, but the accent made Michael think that the man was perhaps French-Canadian.

"Uh, I was looking for Lance Corporal David Brown's footlocker," Michael responded. "He wanted me to retrieve something to take back to his folks in Exeter. It seems that the locker was lost in the fire."

A quiet pause filled the room as both men pondered their next words. Michael was already looking and feeling a bit sheepish that he was wanting to retrieve something from a dead man's locker. The French-Canadian soldier ran his hand over his black crew-cut hair as he looked around the room as if in search of something, and Michael carefully watched to see where the man's eyes finally landed.

"Oh, yes! There it is over there," the soldier said, pointing to a pile of things on the far side of the room. "We had pulled everyone's belongings away from the flames, but we couldn't save everything."

Michael walked slowly to the other side of the room. His legs felt like lead as he dragged each foot forward. The slippers from the infirmary were soiled with soot and grime from the water-soaked ground. He reached the locker and opened it. David had been a trusting spirit and had always kept his locker open for his friends to enjoy the goodies from home. Inside the locker was nothing but David's personal effects. The contents were askew, as if someone had already pilfered through the footlocker.

Everyone had known that the lower part of the locker was private and was not to be opened or disturbed. Michael pulled the tray out that separated the lower part and saw a cache of letters, paperback books, and David's gold verger ring, as well as a scented handkerchief with a red lipstick kiss upon it. Michael replaced the tray and exhaled deeply. Discouraged, he looked down. There, next to the footlocker, was a pair of burnt boots.

Michael remembered David's request, that the small box was stuffed inside a boot. He had said to trust no one else. Michael looked over his shoulder to see where the French-Canadian soldier was. The other soldier had continued on with his job, which Michael decided must have been identifying and sorting through the mess. Michael watched him for a moment, and the soldier continued his work with small glances at Michael as if to see what he was doing. Michael knew that the four soldiers killed in the ISIS assault were most likely being prepped for the long journey home. Their personal items had to be tagged and boxed up to be sent home with them, so he knew the soldier would be busy for at least a short while.

Michael turned back to the footlocker and boots in front him. He was beginning to get incredibly sleepy. The pain medication had begun to do its job, and he was going down hard. He grabbed the burnt boots. Inside one of the boots down near the boot's toe was a wadded-up undershirt. Carefully, Michael pulled the charred shirt from boot and quickly unwrapped it. Inside was a very small wooden box, just a tad bit larger than an engagement ring box. It was ornately carved, and it was the kind of box one would find in an antique store. Michael thought that it was perhaps Moroccan or Middle Eastern because it was adorned with delicate patterns and shapes.

"This is it," Michael said to himself.

"I see you found the damaged boots." The French-Canadian soldier was close behind him.

Michael secretively put the small box into his robe pocket as he stood up. At that very moment, he stumbled, and the lid of the locker fell closed with a loud crash.

"Are you all right, sir?" asked the soldier, stepping forward and placing his hand on Michael's shoulder to steady him.

"Help me back to the infirmary, soldier," Michael said, steadying himself on the wall in front of him. He turned towards the French-Canadian soldier. "I've had enough for today."

"I have you, sir. Looks like you must be on the list to head back with Brown and the other lads who fell. I hope you found what you were looking for."

The soldier placed his arm behind Michael's back and walked him back across the room and out the door to the parade ground. As they made their way across the open area, he spied into Michael's robe pocket and noticed the small box that the American had taken and was trying to hide. He opened the door to the infirmary and helped Michael inside.

An hour later, the French-Canadian soldier received a text message on his personal cellphone.

The text was in code and read: "Have you picked up dinner?"

He texted back a simple response to indicate it would be later: "*Non. Plus tard!*"

CHAPTER 6: THE MOMENT

France, 1513

King Henry had mixed feelings about his victory over the French Knights. The Battle of the Spurs had been a quick and profitable battle as far as its propaganda value. The old witch had warned him not to harm the Dark Knights, however, for their magic was one she wasn't prepared to counter. So, with that and a pit in his stomach, Henry praised his men for their glorious victory and their ill-gotten trophies of noblemen's armor, helmets, swords, and even teeth. Many English soldiers pried out the teeth of the captured, and some of the dead even had their heads cracked open so the victors could extract molars.

A small handful of men who stood close to Henry as bodyguards did not participate in the grisly harvest for gold, armor, and teeth with their fellow soldiers. These men had honor and obediently followed their king to keep him safe from battle. Henry adored this group of men as a father would his sons.

Henry's love for these soldiers granted them a special title: macemen. This guild represented the honor of his court and would forever be marked as the king's own. The leader of the macemen was a large, stout fellow named John Porter. Porter, who was two meters tall, looked impressive on his large warhorse as one of Henry's bodyguards. During a previous battle by his king's side, Porter's shield had raised instinctively, or had been magically manipulated by an unseen force, to just the right position to stop a crossbowman's deadly dart from killing King Henry.

As the army began to make camp that late afternoon, Henry called John Porter to his tent. As Porter entered the tent, Henry beckoned to him from the large chair he sat upon near the back of the tent. Porter crossed the tent and stood before his king, his helmet held in his arm against his chest. Henry nodded and began to speak.

"John Porter, you and your men have shown great restraint and honor in this battle, as you have in many before. As such, I call upon you to stand watch over your king. You and your men will be my personal guard wherever I go. You will also protect the churches and its bishops and priests."

Porter knelt down before his king. "It will be our honor, Your Highness. Our lives are yours to command."

Henry stood up and stepped forward. He reached out his hand and touched Porter's shoulder.

"I cannot knight you, John. Not yet, anyway. But I will bestow upon you your title as a maceman, Keeper of the Faith, Protector of the King and Church, and you will forever have my thanks and devotion."

Porter remained kneeling, but he looked up and asked, "My men will follow you until death. Sire, what will you call us?"

"I will call you the Porters. Yes," Henry said, nodding, "that will be your guild name. However, it must remain church-like. Instead of maces and swords, you will carry ceremonial staffs or rods. The bishops will complain, but once they see the services you provide, they will accept you."

Henry released John's shoulder and motioned for him to stand. As the large man stood, Henry smiled. "The monks who speak Latin will call you '*vergers*,' which means 'stick' or 'one who carries a staff.' Pay them no mind. You might even like the name. I like our language better than Latin, but your guild will probably end up being known as the Vergers."

CHAPTER 7: THE BEGINNING OF THE CURSE

England, 1547

Henry VIII's bedroom was ornately decorated from floor to ceiling in rich tapestries and paintings. The floor was covered with well-worn carpets across the cold stone and wood. Frayed paths in the rug were made from the intense pacing of His Majesty when, many years before, he had been in better health and many pounds heavier, and his only concerns had been about matters of state and love.

On the carpet stood an immense four-poster bed. The immaculately carved wood of the furniture's frame housed maroon and gold decorated bed curtains. Designed to keep its occupant warm during chilly nights, those curtains were pulled back to allow His Majesty more visibility in his chamber per his request.

"Vikings! They are coming! Save my body!" screamed His Majesty in his darkened royal bedchamber as the two doctors at his bedside looked on in painful despair.

The king's failing health had been steadily declining to a point that all recovery to full health had been lost. His voice grew weaker each time he cried out against some phantom foe in the dark. As he scanned his bedroom, the king searched in vain for the Nordic invaders that haunted his dreams. Sensing shadows in his bedroom, he peered into every corner of the room.

His blouse was stained in sweat and body oils. No longer able to keep any of his meals of soft palpable porridge down, remnants of his last meal lay clumped in horribly soiled patterns across his chest and on the sheets. His face was wretched with worry as he again tried to scan for the enemy.

"He's dying, you know?" whispered one of the spindly doctors who then stood near the foot of the bed at its side. "I'd say by tomorrow we will know his condition completely."

"Come, let's leave him be for now," commanded the other physician.

As the two frail men of what was still a science of guesses and potions left the king's chambers, they passed two of Henry's guards at the door.

The verger on the left side of the door held out his staff and stopped the two physicians. "Excuse me, sirs. What's that all about in there? About the Vikings attacking?"

The two physicians looked at each other cautiously and then back to the large guard and the staff before them. The verger lowered his staff as the other guard stepped in front of the men, blocking their path to leave.

"Your king is dying, and he has become delusional," answered one of the physicians. He looked at the other physician and then back to the two vergers before him. "If you have prayers for him, better get on with it before it's too late."

The two vergers nodded and stepped aside to allow the doctors to leave. As the frail physicians scurried away down the corridor, the two large guards looked inside to see their commander. The room was darkly lit, but both soldiers could see their king. Henry's arms were waving back and forth as if trying to catch something.

The soldiers crept in closer to see what was going on.

"Come here, Caesar! Stop flying around and come here!" Henry said aloud to himself.

The guards looked about and saw no creature, nor the bird that the king was making reference to.

"That's it, Caesar," Henry said, holding his arm out before him. "Sit on my arm. Good boy. Can you talk yet?"

The two guards became baffled and scared that their king was talking nonsense.

"Let's get out of here," the verger who had used his staff to stop the physicians said, shaking his head. "He's talking to a ghost or something."

The two men turned and hurried towards the door.

While the guards had been inside the royal bedchamber and not watching the door, an ethereal mist had flowed through the entranceway and into a dark corner of the king's bedroom. The soldiers had not seen the intruder sneak in. To the naked eye, it was if someone had blown out a large candle, and the smoke carried by the wind wafted in any direction that it pleased. It had no smell and made no sound, but it was, indeed, real and waited patiently until the guards left.

CHAPTER 8: PIZZA NIGHT IN ENGLAND

England, 2014

Michael stepped off the British transport plane and onto the tarmac. He had received a two-week pass to recover from his wounds. The air had a brisk spring feel to it as he pulled his coat tighter to his chest. The British airbase was an orchestrated procession of precision and utter chaos. With the English forces withdrawing from Afghanistan, several air transports landed each day.

Michael walked briskly off the tarmac and into the terminal. He looked around and spotted the bright red hair of his friend Tommy through the crowd. Tommy had been accompanied by his new friend Bernard. They were both from the technical institute that was designing the newest British army drone system, called BADS for short. Michael caught Tommy's attention and waved. Slowly, he inched forward with the crowd towards where Tommy and Bernard were waiting across the large room.

Tommy was a cocky one and had that wild adventurer look in his eyes. Always in motion, Tommy was the veritable tempest in a tea cup or, in another way, a rugby match in a beer mug. He was eager in anything he wanted to do. That was why he was very successful at working with computers and programming.

Bernard, on the other hand, relied heavily on his European looks. His full head of wavy black hair matched his olive skin. That mane made him irresistible to all of the female staff at the office. The pronounced dark mole above his lip highlighted his face. He sported a pair of glasses to add to his attire. He was the calm to Tommy's brashness, and he knew it made him look good. Confident of success, he remained quiet and shy-like until he was ready to strike.

Finally, Michael reached his friends through the thinning crowd. He smiled broadly as he extended his hand to Tommy. "Good to see you!"

Tommy took his friend's hand and shook it vigorously. "So glad you're home, Michael. We heard about that last attack on the advance base. Lots of good soldiers lost their lives."

Tommy released Michael's hand as Michael nodded and shut his eyes for a moment.

"Yeah, my friend David died there as well," Michael responded sadly.

"We heard," Bernard said, stepping forward and placing his hand on Michael's shoulder. He smiled encouragingly, his natural charm and calmness coming through. "That's why we have a surprise for you in the car. Come on then. Let's get you signed out. Tommy parked the car right outside so we can make a quick getaway."

Bernard chuckled as he patted Michael on the back, and Michael and Tommy joined in. They walked over to join the line to complete the papers for Michael's R&R.

Once he had signed the last paper, Michael followed his buddies from the terminal to the waiting car. Tommy pressed a button on his keys, and the doors unlocked. Tommy slid into the driver's seat, and Bernard walked around the car and got in the passenger side. Michael opened the door and climbed into the back seat. True enough, there was a basket filled with wonderful gifts on the other seat, including sandwich meats, cheeses, and, above all, a few pints of ale. Michael tossed his bag onto the floorboard and closed the door. He reached over and picked up a card that was inside the basket. He opened the card and read it. It had been signed by all the employees at BADS.

"You guys are so awesome," Michael said, putting the card back in the envelope and placing it in the basket. "Thank you!"

"No problem," Tommy said, turning in the seat to look at Michael.

Michael looked through the gifts and found a cellphone and a charger that worked in English outlets. He held it up. "What's this?"

Bernard shifted in his seat to look at Michael as well. He smiled broadly. "It is yours to use while you are in England. It has a message on it that I think you will want to hear."

"I contacted your mom and dad through the employee wellness program at work and told them we were going to help you here in England. They were very happy that we could help," added Tommy.

Michael turned on the phone and navigated to the messages section on the phone.

Bernard turned back around in his seat and began texting on his phone as Michael fiddled with the buttons and played back the message on speakerphone. A familiar voice began to speak. "Hello, brother, it's me, Steve. Elizabeth and I will be on a flight to England to see you soon and help with your recovery. Mom and Dad are worried sick about you and wanted us to come and convince you to come home—this time for good."

Michael held back tears as he listened to his brother on the recording.

In the background of the recording, his cousin Elizabeth's voice chimed in. "Hello, cousin! Are there any good-looking English chaps there for you to introduce me to?"

Bernard looked up from his texting, and he and Tommy both looked at Michael and grinned as if they should be considered as potential candidates.

Michael chuckled and shook his head as he pressed the button to stop listening to the message. "At ease, boys. Elizabeth is still seeing my friend Jack. It's an on-again, off-again relationship. She's just wanting a nice person to show her around."

"I'm a nice person," Bernard blurted out as he adjusted his silver-rimmed glasses on his nose. his head buried again in a texting conversation on his cellphone.

"I am, too," added Tommy. He held up his keys and shook them. "And I will show her around London."

"Not before me!" said Bernard, glancing over at Tommy with a smile.

"Fellas!" Michael said sharply as he opened an ale and took a long swig from the bottle.

The car started up, and Tommy looked over his shoulder. "So, Michael, where do you want to go first?"

Michael finished another long drink of ale and wiped the side of his mouth with the back of his hand. A wide smile spread across his face. "Anywhere there is a pizza night!"

CHAPTER 9: THE HORN AND THE HOUND PUB

England, 2014

Michael, Tommy, and Bernard were in heaven. There was nothing like fresh baked pizza right out of a century-old wood-fired oven originally designed to bake breads, and the gastro pub was a fun and trendy hangout at night for the likes of the three young men. The ale was delicious, and the patrons seemed content.

Michael and his friends occupied the second semi-circular booth near the front door where they were finishing up their pizzas. Michael looked around the dimly lit room with its white walls stained with ages of dust and grease. Random pieces of soccer memorabilia sat here and there on dusty shelves. There were soccer trophies, a ball, and what appeared to be a jersey from some local team. On a shelf behind the bar was a picture frame that was unceremoniously draped with an orange-colored bra.

"What's up with that?" Michael asked, pointing to the unusual display.

Tommy and Bernard glanced towards where Michael was pointing. Bernard chuckled but his mouth was full of food. Tommy smiled and nodded. With his mouth half-full, he said, "The picture is of a local soccer hero from the 90s, but nobody knows how the bra got there."

Michael shook his head and smiled, imaging the possibilities.

A television above the wood-paneled bar was tuned to an international news agency, and the broadcaster was talking about the recent events in Afghanistan. A rowdy cheer quickly broke apart from the normal pub din as everyone cheered to the images of British combat units firing back at the enemy. Fresh pints of ale were passed around to anyone that looked as though they were still in the army. One soldier on crutches, who was still recovering from a shrapnel wound to his ankle, was quickly patted on the back and toasted for being a brave hero.

Bernard looked to Michael and asked, "How was it over there?"

"It was really great that I got to meet many of your countrymen," Michael replied and then stuffed his last bite of pizza into his mouth. He chewed for a moment before continuing. "I believe we have the upper hand with our drone technology, and the artillery unit I was attached to made great use of my Wolf."

"Your 'wolf'?" asked Tommy as he finished up his pizza and pushed his plate towards the center of the table.

"Yeah, my drone. I built a submarine when I was in high school, and I called her Wolf. So, the legend continues." Michael smiled and took a long drink of beer.

"Hey, look over there," Bernard nodded towards the bar as he pushed away his plate with its last bite of pizza. "Those three birds by the bar are gawking at us."

Michael and Tommy glanced across the room at the three girls who were huddled together whispering and looking their way. The girl in the group with glasses blushed when she saw the guys looking at her and turned towards the bar. The auburn-haired girl snapped a selfie of herself with puckered lips and then turned it around and waved it towards the boys, causing a broad smile to spread over Tommy's face. The dark-haired one raised her eyebrows and pointed towards Michael with a long red acrylic nail and waggled her finger.

"I think one of them has her eyes on our Michael," Bernard said and chuckled. He shook his head. "Damn, Yank! You get all the girls hot and bothered with that American accent you have."

"Me," Michael said, almost choking on his mouthful of beer. "I didn't do shit. It's Tommy with that red hair of his. Maybe the girls think he's a brash Viking come to take his bride!"

Tommy wadded up a napkin from the table and tossed it into Michael's face in protest as Michael and Bernard laughed.

"Watch it, fellows," whispered Bernard, shifting in his chair and composing himself. "Here they come."

Michael and Tommy straightened as the three girls walked up to the table.

"Hello, boys," purred the dark-haired leader of the group with the long nails. She was dressed in a cheesy leopard-print zip-up top with a sheep-lined vest and cheap blue jeans that she had worn way too many times. "What you three up to, eh? Care for some company?"

The other two girls giggled and elbowed each other as the three boys all went a little red in the face.

"Move over, handsome. Let me sit next to you," the leader of the three girls said as she slid into the booth and made herself comfortable next to Michael.

The other two girls stood staring down at Bernard and giggling until he smiled awkwardly and stood up to let them in. The auburn-haired girl slid across the booth's brown fake leather and pressed herself in close to Tommy. As the girl with glasses slid in next, the auburn-haired girl pressed her cheek up against Tommy's and snapped a selfie. Bernard slid in next to the girl with glasses, but it was a really tight fit with six of them in the curved booth.

The dark-haired girl next to Michael pulled out a pack of cigarettes and offered one to everyone at the table. When no one accepted, she shrugged and pulled a cigarette from the pack. She pulled a lighter out of the half-empty cigarette box and flicked it, inhaling deeply as she lit the cigarette. She leaned her head back and exhaled a large cloud of greyish smoke. She held the cigarette out to Michael, but he shook his head.

"Hey! You can't smoke in here!" yelled the bartender from behind the bar.

"Up yours!" responded the dark-haired girl, glaring at the portly bartender.

The bartender made a move towards the end of the bar, and the dark-haired girl rolled her eyes as she leaned towards the center of the table and crushed the cigarette out in the last bite of pizza Bernard had left on his plate. "Aw, you can't have any fun these days, what with the PC police everywhere."

"It's all right, miss," responded Michael, hoping that she wouldn't make a scene. "I don't smoke."

"Very well. My name is Rachel," the dark-haired girl said, turning towards Michael and rubbing her shoulder up against his.

The bartender shook his head and mumbled something under his breath as he headed back to where he had been pouring drinks. Michael exhaled deeply, relieved that things seemed to be under control.

"This is Sara," Rachel said as she pointed a thin finger with its long red nail towards the quiet girl with the glasses. She then pointed to the auburn-haired girl who was taking another selfie. "And that's Cynthia. What's your names, eh?"

"Pleased to meet you all. My name is Michael. I'm an American. That over there is Bernard, and that's Tommy."

Hellos were exchanged all around and a waitress came over to clear the table. Tommy ordered a round of beers for everyone, and the waitress brought them back to the table a few minutes later.

Rachel slid closer to Michael and started to rub his leg, but he smiled and caught hold of her hand and sat it in her lap. He patted the back of her hand and then stuffed his hand in his pocket as he nodded at her. She giggled as she wrapped her arm around his shoulders. Using her long fingernails, she stroked Michael's short, dark hair. "So, what brings you to England, dearie? Come looking for a good time?"

Michael rolled his eyes and forced a smile. "Just here for a couple of weeks."

"What'd you do to yourself?" she asked as she pointed to the bandage on his neck with a long red nail.

"Just a flesh wound," Michael said, reaching up and pulling her arm from around his shoulder. He looked over at Tommy, who laughed.

Bernard was seated next to the quiet girl with glasses named Sara. He was behaving goofy, like he had never seen a girl, much less talked to one. He kept staring at his hands in his lap, and Sara just smiled and slid her glasses back up her nose whenever he glanced up.

Cynthia leaned in towards Sara and held her arm out in front of her with her phone. "Come on. Let's take a shot for my online fans."

"No, thanks," Bernard said as he held up his hand and turned his face so she couldn't get a picture of him.

"Hey, what's up with hiding your handsome face?" asked Cynthia as she brushed back her auburn hair with her fingers. "You're acting like you are some movie star hiding incognito."

Bernard kept his hand up to shield his face and shook his head. "I'm just shy, that's all."

Sara took a deep pull on her pint of beer and slid her glasses back up her nose. She looked at Bernard and asked, "How can you be shy with looks like that, my love?"

"Aye, don't bother with 'im," interrupted Tommy as he reached over for a kiss from Cynthia. "If it's looks you want, have a go at me, eh?"

As if on cue, all three girls chuckled and rolled their eyes at the redhead. Bernard dropped his hand and did a silent mouthing of "thank you" to Tommy for getting him out of the tough spot. Tommy, trying to be the smooth one, grinned widely as his arm rounded Cynthia's shoulder in an apparent attempt to rub his hand over her backside. Giggles and laughter rang out from the table of six as everyone settled down to a fun evening of drinking and flirting.

Outside, however, was another party interested in the table of six. A tall and quiet man stood in the alleyway across from the pub. He wore an old grayish coat that could double as a raincoat. It was well-worn and reeked of heavy tobacco smoke. A long black scarf wrapped around the man's neck like a large snake strangling its next meal. His black hair was curly and unkempt, and his five-day-old beard made him look the sinister part that he actually played.

The gaunt man's name was Claude Vonyou, a hired thug from France whose paycheck depended on getting what his employers back in France wanted him to steal, or kill for and then take. The mission, whatever the cost, was to get the box that had belonged to the British soldier, then in the hands of the American Vonyou watched. It had to be retrieved. That was his mission.

Vonyou knew that all he had to do was to wait for the right moment and seize the opportunity to get the package. He also knew if the American made it back to an army base, it would be practically impossible to infiltrate, whether American or British. The best time to kill him would be before he got to the safety of a camp.

Vonyou's employers had been very secretive as to why they wanted that box and its contents, but they had been just as determined that failure was not an option. Vonyou's very existence depended on his success. Such motivational conditions would drive a normal hitman crazy with distrust and fear, but it was nothing new for Vonyou.

He checked his pistol with the eight-inch silencer on it. The gun Vonyou used had always found its mark. It was getting colder, and it was time for another one of his *Gauloisses*, a French cigarette brand that had been around for decades. Instantly recognizable by its hyper-strong sour tobacco odor, the smell of the very strong cigarette reminded one of a burning wet rope. As for Vonyou, it was the brand his family had smoked and he had grown up with. If anything, the smoke comforted Vonyou and kept him warm as he waited for the American to come out.

CHAPTER 10: WHAT GOES IN, MUST COME OUT

England, 2014

Inside the pub, Michael was beginning to feel the stress of combat fading away as he grew more comfortable with the night's festivities. However, he was growing tired and had made a silent signal to Bernard and Tommy that it was time to go. Sadly, Michael's driver Tommy was feeling the effects of too much beer, and the affections of a young lady who kept rubbing her leg against his all night.

"Tommy's toast," Michael said underneath his breath, shaking his head.

A quick glance over to Bernard produced the same result. Bernard's eyes were glazed over from too much love or drink as well. The three girls had done their damage and were in the process of dividing and conquering their dates for the evening.

Michael wanted no part of it. He nudged Tommy with his elbow, drawing his attention. "Tommy, I'm going to get out of here. You guys stay and have fun. I'll meet you back at your flat."

Michael had stayed with Tommy the last time he was in England, and he was sure that he could walk there since they had passed it on their way to the bar. Tommy's apartment wasn't that great, but it did have a pull-out bed from an old couch. Michael was to crash there until his cousin Elizabeth and brother Steve arrived the next day.

Tommy shook his head. Slightly slurring, he said, "Stay! The fun is just beginning."

Michael looked at the others, but no one else seemed to notice their conversation. "I'll be all right. I just need some sleep. I'll see you guys at your flat."

Tommy nodded, distracted by Cynthia as she kissed his cheek, and slipped his keys out of his pocket and into Michael's awaiting hand.

Michael stuffed the keys into his pocket, relieved that having them meant his inebriated friends would also have to walk home. He turned to Rachel, who was finishing up another beer. "Mind if I get out?"

"Where are you going, handsome?" Rachel asked as she slid out of the booth. She giggled, thinking he must be headed to the wash closet.

"I've got to get going. I'm calling it a day."

"You can't leave. Who's going to keep me company?" Rachel protested in disappointment as she held on to the table to steady herself.

"Don't worry. These guys will keep you company."

As Michael stood, a soft moan emanated from the three girls at the thought that the best-looking man was leaving. Rachel slid back into the booth and tried to pull him back towards the table to sit next to her, but he gently broke free.

"Sorry, Rachel. I know Tommy and Bernard will take good care of you." Michael winked at his friends. Tommy winked back, and Bernard nodded his head.

Everyone said good-bye, and Michael turned and walked over to the bar where he asked the barman where the WC was so he could relieve himself before the long walk to Tommy's apartment. The man pointed down a dimly lit wooden hallway.

The bathroom had seen its better days. It stank of stale cigarettes where patrons snuck a smoke, hidden from the barkeeper's wrath. The other annoying smell was of urine. There were no stalls, just urinals and one toilet. Michael relieved himself in one of the urinals. It was strangely quiet on that side of the bar. He could barely hear the patrons in the main area drinking and laughing.

The only light in the restroom was in the ceiling, an old long fluorescent tube that buzzed and flicked as if it had a life of its own. The constant on-again and off-again of the light was as if some tiny gremlin had his claw on the switch and turned it off and on just to unravel Michael's nerves.

Almost finished with the task of relieving himself, Michael heard the door behind him slowly open. Whether it was his military training or remembering days of old when playing hide and go seek with his younger brother, he instantly recognized the distinct sound of a squeaky door slowly opening.

Michael froze, with a touch of fear, as he was in a difficult position. If he turned to face the person coming in, he would urinate on the floor and his pants. If he waited, his back would be exposed to a possible attack.

"Who's there?" he asked, glancing over his shoulder as best he could.

The fluorescent bulb flickered again and added to the suspense as another round of off and on with the light in the bathroom ensued.

The door continued to swing open, and a hand slowly appeared around the door. The hand moved to the light switch next to the door and made a quick flick to turn the light off.

By this time, Michael had begun to zip up his pants and was about to turn and face what he knew must be an attacker. *This is it*, he thought.

"I got you!" said a voice as arms swung around and grabbed Michael from both sides.

The smell of tobacco and beer was atrocious. The sickening sweet smell of vomit attacked Michael's nostrils, leading him to believe that his attacker must have thrown up earlier.

Michael let out a faint breath of fear, but he quickly recovered and executed a defensive maneuver that broke the attacker's bear hug and reversed the hold to where he had the attacker disarmed and immobilized. Strangely, the attacker had long hair and didn't put up much of a defense.

"Hey! That hurts! I didn't know you were so rough," Rachel said.

'Rachel! Do not ever sneak up on a soldier like that. You could have gotten yourself hurt or even killed."

"I know, I'm sorry, but I wanted to kiss you goodnight," she responded as she was released from her hold.

Michael felt along the wall and turned the light back on. Drunk and in a stupor, Rachel was a wreck. Her mascara had run down her cheeks which added to her clown-like features with the leopard-print top and cheap jeans. Her top was covered in stains and vomit. She had one shoe off, and as to the location of the other, only the barman would know in the morning when he cleaned up his pub.

Michael took Rachel by the arm and guided her out of the men's room and back down the hallway and to the front door. Next, he eased Rachel out the pub's door with one hand around her waist. He wanted her to get some fresh air. Rachel held on tightly to Michael for balance. Then, when she felt more stabilized, her hand made its way to Michael's buttocks for a quick squeeze. The cold air assaulted her face with a sting, and she quickly came to her senses. Michael propped her up against the pub's front windowsill.

The barman came out to check on the two and brought Rachel's missing shoe and a glass of water. He passed the glass to Rachel and then looked at Michael. "Are you two okay?"

"Yes, I'm fine sir," Michael said. He reached over to grab Rachel as she swayed and spilt some water on the sidewalk. "But this young lady needs to go home with her friends. A taxi would probably be in order."

"I'm good… I'm good. Let's go back inside for another round," said Rachel, waving her free hand. She swayed again, and Michael caught her and propped her back up straight.

Michael looked at her face and pulled out a handkerchief from his pocket. He tried to wipe away some of the tears and smudged mascara. For a brief moment, he felt sorry for her and her condition. Rachel sipped some of the water and then offered the glass to Michael to hold.

"I'll get the others and call a taxi," the portly barman said and opened the door.

Michael nodded. "Thanks."

The barman went back inside to gather Rachel's friends to send them home. He walked over to their table and pulled the bottles from the table.

"Hey! What do you think you're doing?" Tommy protested.

The barman ignored Tommy. "Okay, ladies, time to go. Your other friend is so pissed she can't stand, and she can't make it on her own. Gather your things and hers, too."

Tommy knew it was no use to argue. He quickly wrote down his phone number on a beer coaster and gave it to Cynthia. She took it with a smile and said, "I'll call you."

Sara pushed her glasses up her nose and seized the opportunity to grab Bernard by the hair and gave him a fat, wet kiss goodbye. Speechless, Bernard sat there in silence for a moment, dumbfounded. He had never been kissed liked that, and he didn't even know what to do next. He was still only able to mutter a soft goodbye as he slid out of the booth for Sara and Cynthia to get out. As Sara stood up, she put a napkin with her cellphone number on it into his pocket.

The barman escorted the girls to the door and held it open as the entourage processed out. The two laughed and giggled as if they had scored the winning goal at a soccer match. Sara even kissed the portly barman on his cheek which, in turn, made him blush. The barman turned and went back inside where Bernard and Tommy waved him over to pay their tab.

Rachel was standing on her own by that point, but Michael remained close by to catch her if she fell. The air was cold, and the smells of the city were in the wind, cigarette smoke, sausages on a grill somewhere, beer, urine, and even a peculiar burning smell that was very strong and emanated from across the street in the pitch-black alley. The night was still in full swing on that side of town.

"Whoops! I dropped my phone somewhere," Rachel slurred, looking down at the sidewalk.

Michael, standing on the curb facing the bar window and Rachel, quickly noticed the dropped cellphone and knelt down to pick it up.

Suddenly, a bullet smashed into Rachel's forehead, the very same spot where Michael's head had been a split second earlier. Her head was violently thrown backwards into the bar window as the kinetic energy of the round impacted her skull.

"*Merde!*" whispered Vonyou as he quickly tried to make his escape through the back part of the alley. His smoldering Gauloisses cigarette lay burning on the cobblestone street.

"Take cover!" shouted Michael as he grabbed the other two girls and pulled them to the ground. He knew the sounds and sights of war, and someone was shooting at them.

The girls huddled against the wall looking around, not knowing what to do next. They glanced over to see their dead friend lying motionless and still. Her blouse was covered in blood as the head wound had gushed crimson to the beat of her dying heart. She had been dead by the time she hit the ground. The bullet was still inside her skull, but the pub's glass window had a spider-like shatter to it where Rachel's head had bounced against it.

Inside the pub, Tommy and Bernard had jumped out of the booth and headed for the door. Tommy opened the door to let everyone back inside. "Get in here!"

Michael pushed Cynthia and Sara towards the door, and they crawled along the sidewalk into the pub. Michael dragged Rachel's body and followed them into the bar for safety. Once everyone was safely inside, Tommy locked the door.

Behind the bar, the barman had made it to the telephone and called the police. Michael and his friends were in a quiet stupor as to why someone had been shooting, much less had killed someone. Michael gently lay Rachel's bloodied head and body on the floor. He took off his light jacket and draped it over Rachel's body out of respect. In the distance, sirens could be heard as the police were on their way.

CHAPTER 11: CORRECTIONS AND NEW ORDERS

England, 2014

"Report!" demanded a deep French voice over Vonyou's cellphone.

"My shot missed and killed a bystander. I wanted Cotter dead so that in the confusion I could act as a helper and pick his pocket for the box. He moved the instant I fired, and now everyone has scrambled inside. I will now have to follow him and catch him by surprise."

"No! Kill everyone inside and take that box. Whatever it takes, get that box!" responded the man on the other end of the cellphone before the call disconnected.

Vonyou had moved himself to a new position on the rooftop above the alleyway to watch the aftermath. He slid the cellphone into his coat pocket and checked his gun and ammunition. He moved to the back of the rooftop and climbed down the metal ladder that led to the alley that adjoined the one he had been watching Michael from earlier in the evening. He slipped stealthily down the alley and surveyed his target.

As he exited the alleyway and began to cross the street to move towards the pub, a pair of headlights turned the corner of the street and illuminated Vonyou entirely. Like a deer in the headlights, he bolted back into the shadows and faded away into the night, knowing that his plans were spoiled as he heard the wail of approaching sirens. The source of the lights was the black taxi cab that was en route to pick up Rachel and the girls.

The police arrived next in three cars with their blue lights flashing and sirens wailing. A total of six officers got out and began to secure and cordon off the area. Other police units could be heard responding as well. An ambulance pulled up on the other side of the street. The medics were already aware that they were retrieving a body. The gurney had a temporary body bag already unfolded and ready for its new occupant.

The senior police officer entered the pub and began the process of interrogating everyone as to what had happened and who was involved. Michael introduced himself as a lieutenant in the US Army and explained that he was on military leave.

By that time, the ambulance team had begun putting Rachel's body into the black body bag. Michael's coat was about to be zipped up inside the bag until Michael told them that it was his coat. He gently squeezed his jacket that was covered in Rachel's blood to make sure that the special box was inside a pocket. It was, and he transferred it to an empty pants pocket.

Outside the pub, a policeman with dark hair and a mustache began to question the cabby, "As you were approaching the scene, did you see anything unusual?"

The round-bellied cabby lifted his cap and ran his hand across his balding scalp. "So, I drove around the corner of Coker Street, and there he was, like a shadow of evil. His overcoat flew in the wind like a raven's wing. He looked at me as if I was disturbing him. He turned and ran down that alley there."

As the mustached officer finished taking the cabby's statement, a thin officer walked over to the place where the cabby had indicated and found a burnt-out cigarette butt that still reeked strongly in the dark alley. With a set of investigation latex gloves, he picked up the butt and put it into an evidence bag and went to report his findings to his superior inside.

"Sir," the thin officer said, holding up the evidence bag, "look at this. Our shooter might be French."

"All right. Box it up for a DNA check with our database. Maybe our Frenchie has been a bad boy elsewhere," replied the officer in charge.

For the next hour and a half, the police took the statements of the witnesses in the bar, including the barman, Tommy, Bernard, Cynthia, and Sara. They collected contact information on all the witnesses. They searched the area but were unable to find the possibly French gunman. Eventually, the officer in charge allowed everyone inside to leave.

When Bernard, Tommy, and Michael were excused, they proceeded to their car. Michael, still being the soberest one in the group, opted to drive back to Tommy's apartment. Once there, they began to unwind from the horrible night. Tommy flopped down onto the recliner, Bernard went to the bathroom with his cellphone in hand, and Michael went to the kitchen to get some water.

"I can't believe that girl is dead," said Tommy, leaning his head back against the recliner and looking up at the ceiling.

"Yeah, she was right there beside me when the bullet flew over my head," Michael called from the kitchen. "For a moment there, I thought I was back 'in country.'"

Tommy closed his eyes for a moment, but the sound of muffled talking unnerved him after the night's events.

"Bernard? Hey, where did you go?" asked Tommy. He got up from the recliner and walked down the hallway towards the bathroom, stopping outside the locked bathroom door. "Are you in there? Sounds like you're talking to someone."

Seconds later, Bernard emerged from the bathroom only to find his friend Tommy leaning against the door. Tommy stumbled backwards.

"What were you doing in there?" Tommy smiled slyly. "Were you calling that girl Sara that kissed you at the pub?"

Tommy gently shoved Bernard to the wall to press him for more details. Bernard shrugged off his friend's playful assault and proceeded to the kitchen for a bottle of something cold. Michael was refilling his water glass as Bernard came in. Placing his phone next to the sink, Bernard opened the fridge to get a beer. The bottle opener was in a drawer on the other side of the refrigerator.

"Piss off, Tommy!" Bernard said with a grin.

"Aww, don't get quiet on me. You were talking to someone in the bathroom. Was it her?" Tommy pried, standing in the doorway of the kitchen.

Michael walked over and patted Bernard on the shoulder and gave him an assuring wink. "It's all right. She was pretty."

While Bernard was distracted, Tommy snuck into the kitchen and grabbed Bernard's cellphone from the countertop. He turned it on before Bernard realized what was happening.

"Hey! Your last call started with the international code 33, a French phone number." Tommy looked at Bernard, a bewildered expression on his face. "Is Sara French?"

"Ah, *oui, oui!*" laughed Michael.

"Give me that bloody phone!" Bernard darted across the room and snatched the phone from Tommy's hand. "Don't you ever do that again!"

"Calm down, calm down...," said Tommy, throwing his hands up in surrender.

Bernard looked angrily at his friend and nodded his head. A thick pall of silence filled the kitchen with an unsettling feeling.

"Why don't we get ready for bed?" Michael suggested. "It's been quite the day, and I think we could all use a good night's sleep."

Bernard continued to glare at Tommy. Michael walked over and placed his hand on Bernard's shoulder, making him jump.

"Hey, let's call it a night," Michael said, removing his hand from Bernard's shoulder. "We'll all feel better in the morning."

Bernard and Tommy both nodded. Tommy headed to his bedroom and passed out on his bed with his clothes still on. Bernard took his beer and went to the guest room in an angry funk, and Michael crashed on the pullout couch. The small wooden box was safely under the throw pillow beneath his head. The next day, he would travel to the Essex Cathedral and return David's box and fulfill his promise.

CHAPTER 12: PALACE OF WHITEHALL

London, January 1547

Henry's candlelit bedroom was filled with dignitaries, courtiers, messengers, and priests. The mysterious smoke-like mist was also there, but it hid in the shadows. No one knew of its presence as the thick gray candle smoke of the dozen or so other candles hid the wisps of the semi-ethereal presence. It listened carefully as the king made his final moments count.

Henry lay motionless due to utter exhaustion as his breathing slowed with every minute. A priest came closer and leaned over Henry. "My lord, do you wish to make a last confession?"

Henry's eyes fluttered open, and he took a haggard breath. "I call as my witness… Christ the Lord… who will be my judge, that I repent my transgression and dealings… outside my faith. I denounce the witch… Cassandra… and confess all of my sins unto God."

"Liar!" hissed the smoke-like shadow from the corner of the room.

Everyone in the room froze with fear. With a fast wave of its hand, the apparition cast a spell which made each person perfectly still. Even the guards outside the bedroom stood absolutely still. When the ethereal creature felt completely certain that everyone was affected by the spell, it drifted towards Henry's bedside. The king's face was in a half-sneer.

The smoke-like mist of the intruder began to swirl into a column. The column took form. The form became humanlike and was made solid. A second later, Cassandra appeared beside the king's bed.

The king looked scared, and it pleased her. It proved she still had a hold on the dying king. She stretched out her old wrinkled hand like a dried sunflower stalk and touched Henry's forehead. Her dry skin scratched his forehead as she wiped away a drop of sweat and licked the moisture to taste his mortality. He awoke from her spell with a start and strained his eyes to look at her.

"Why?" he asked softly.

"You owe me my land," the old witch hissed. "You swore an oath. I have come to collect the debt."

Henry grunted and winced in pain as death was very near. He felt another wave of delirium approaching as the witch watched and waited for her moment of triumph. The enthralled people who had been frozen still were beginning to slowly come out of their spell. Tiny sounds of moans and breathing could be heard. Like a slow thawing of a frozen flower, Cassandra's victims were aware of their spell that kept them still, but they couldn't move nor speak. They listened to what the old witch said as she waved her decrepit hand above Henry's body.

"*Vos imperium meum.* You are mine to control. *Sequetur legio corvorum corpore ossa mea, si non ad aetrnitatem iter.* My legion of crows and ravens will haunt your body and bones for eternity if I do not get my way."

Henry, in his confusion, drew back upon his memories of his childhood. He knew very well those Latin words; he had heard a part of it before from the monastery monks who had educated him when he was a child. The monks had played with the crows in the courtyard as a source of entertainment. Morsels of bread and uncooked meats had been put out for the crows to enjoy. The crows had gathered the bits of food and flown off to some distant part of the woods outside the monastery's confines to eat.

As a child, Henry had thrown pebbles at the monk's crow friends for sport. To surprise his prey, Henry had built straw men and adorned them with a shirt or small jacket to hide in between. He had been able to fool the small black birds, only to get one or two clobbered by one of his small rocks. The crows had constantly cawed their protests in the tree branches and on the ground as Henry had agitated their cozy relationship with the monks.

One of the monks, Abbott, senior to many of the younger initiates, even had kept a raven for a pet. The raven, much larger than his crow cousins, had proudly strutted back and forth along the window ledge as if it had been some noble member of royalty in the *Corvidae* family. It had cawed every now and then as if giving commands or declarations to the crow community.

"*Vos imperium meum,*" Abbott had whispered to his raven. "Tell the crows that you control them."

Henry had actually enjoyed that raven and had given Abbott's large black bird its own name, Caesar. When Abbott had died many years later, believed to be natural causes, the raven Caesar had been given to Henry as a pet. The raven had lived an unusually long life, as most ravens lived to only around 15 years old. Caesar had lived well past that.

Other ravens had been caught by the monks to encourage a breeding program that might yield birds with lifespans similar to Caesar's longevity. The purpose of such a program had been to have long-living ravens who could control the rampaging crows from damaging the valuable crops of nearby fields. Desperate farmers would have been quick to buy or barter with such things as pottery, hams, and even forged tools.

The breeding program, however, had failed from the start as if some outside manipulation had been to blame. The monks' captured ravens continually hatched only "wickedly mean" crows of a larger stature. The lifespan had not improved either, for the ones that had stayed had only lived for seven years. Most of the wicked birds had usually flown away after a season. A true raven could have only been bred from quality stock. As to the fate of those ill-tempered crows which had been bred, no one knew.

In the candlelit sick room filled with heavy smoke, Henry moved restlessly under the covers. His eyes fluttered open, and the image of the withered old witch danced in and out with each movement of his eyelids. He drifted somewhere between reality and remembrance, his mind whirling back to a time long before as his eyes closed.

It had been during the later years in Henry's young adult life when he had met Cassandra. She had been peddling some herbs and dried roots she had harvested to the monks in exchange for bread. The old crone had spied young Henry and asked the young master how his Caesar was. Henry had been astonished that the strange old woman had known of his prize bird and friend.

"Has your young friend learned to write yet?" Cassandra had asked.

"What? My raven? No, he doesn't know how. Leave him be."

Cassandra had reached into her sack and produced a small bottle of a foul-smelling black liquid. It had looked like black pitch, normally used in weatherproofing hemp, but it had been very mellifluous in nature. She had poured the liquid onto a nearby tree stump. The black ooze had spread quickly across the flat surface. She had then raised her staff and tipped it in such a way as if to summon someone. Caesar had flown from Henry's side and landed on top of the stump, his feet getting covered by the black ink.

"Don't hurt him!" Henry had shouted.

"*Vos imperium meum*," Cassandra had chanted as she held out her hand. Her palm had moved in such a fashion as to invite Caesar to move across the stump.

Caesar had cocked his head, his large black beak pointed to Cassandra's nose. He had stood motionless, as if in a trance. Then, he'd cawed loudly and spread his wings and flown back to land on a piece of linen near Henry's side. Caesar had walked on the light-colored cloth, as if to wipe his feet from the ink.

Caesar's motions had left little markings from his claws as he stepped. The marks had begun to change, as if the scratches were floating, moving, joining to make letters. Letters had become words. Words had drawn meaning.

"NO CONTROL CAESAR," the message had read.

"You stupid fool of a bird! You have lived too long with these idiot monks, and now you are protected by this little prince." Cassandra had turned to Henry and hissed, "It was I who gave Abbott that stupid bird. He's as useless now as he was back then. Like all ravens, they don't respect me like my crows do. He will learn, and he will be mine to control again someday. You'll see!"

Cassandra had struck the air with her fist and had vanished from the young Henry's sight in a wisp of dust that sprang up from the ground like a dust devil.

His eyes fluttering open once more, Henry returned from his daydream of remembrance to face the witch once again as she stood at his bedside. His forehead was dripping with sweat, and his mouth was dry.

"No control Caesar," he muttered to Cassandra. "You tried to control the monks through Abbott, but the monks prevailed, as did my raven and his kind after him."

Exhausted beyond recovery, Henry repeated the words "monks, monks, monks" over and over until he slipped into unconsciousness and was no more.

Cassandra, seeing the last of the spell fading away on the people around the king's bed, quickly raised her hand and muttered a final incantation.

"I might not control my lands anymore, but soon I will control those black knights you tried to slaughter. Even now they are forming their own guild, a guild vowed to avenge their brothers. You should have heeded my advice, dead king. Now my crows will join forces with them, and you will never find rest again."

With that, she vanished.

In the silence that followed, the stunned staff came to and approached their king's bed. Indeed, he was gone. Some commented on what they had heard. From incantations to monks, the late king's audience pondered their review.

CHAPTER 13: A TREACHEROUS NIGHT AT THE INN

England, Spring 1547

Henry's body was heavy and needed stout men to carry his casket to the waiting wagon pulled by large draft horses. The trip to Windsor was to be long and arduous. The vergers escorted their king, along with an entourage of the king's court, soldiers, and priests. The travelling band made slow progress with the heavy and bulky transport. Eventually, a local inn was found on the king's road and was a strategic stopping spot for both the men and horses to catch their breath. The very large lead-lined casket with the king's body was brought into the tavern for careful watch.

While Henry's soldiers and entourage gorged themselves on roasted chicken and lamb and drank vast quantities of brown ale from the tavern's large casks, the vergers camped outside. Their life was one of duty and service to the king. To them, life was much simpler. Henry's wars had made them tough and independent. Yet, it was in times of reflection that these men, these vergers, would find solitude, peace, and the grace of God. In their opinion, the church was the king. In serving the church, they would forever serve their master who had recognized their devotion. This was their belief in *"ad regem,"* which in Latin meant "to our king."

Later that night, almost to the new morning, the last of the ale was consumed. Many of the soldiers were asleep either upstairs with the local tavern wenches or downstairs passed out headfirst onto the large tables that were placed on the far side of the great fireplace. The king's casket had started to smell of His Highness inside decomposing. The casket had been placed on the heaviest of the tavern's tables. Still, the immense weight of the casket demanded respect from the table to hold fast. As far as light and warmth, the last of the fires both inside the tavern and outside with the vergers had begun to fade into memory.

Unseen by all, just outside the tavern's side window, was a crow, the smaller and craftier of the birds in the genus of *Corvidae*. This particular crow was female. She had spied on the humans the entire evening. She watched with glee that none of the humans were watching the king's casket. Her friends would be pleased to know such things. For a crow to serve as a spy was one thing, but for the bird to know how, when, and where to attack was entirely another matter. When she was totally satisfied that she had seen enough to make her report, the crow quietly left her secluded branch where she had been hiding and flew into the night to meet up with her new friends, the French Guild.

A mile away and hidden off the main road, the crow, with a small stick held in one of its feet, landed in the grass next to the French Guild's gaunt master. Reynauld the Black was one of the survivors of the massacre by Henry's men. It had been his quick thinking and heavy gauntlet that had struck down that English peasant so that he could get away. His entire existence was to avenge his brothers and pay back the "Grind their bones" insult that Henry had commanded. Reynauld looked down at the crow in weary amusement, his eyes sunken with dark circles beneath them, and asked a simple question. "What did you find, Cassandra?"

The female crow cawed only once and then quickly morphed into the old crone Cassandra. Reynauld's men, their hearts blackened by hate and longing for their honor to be restored whatever the cost, backed away in quick succession as the witchcraft of changing shapes unnerved them still.

"It is as I suspected. They are full of drink and are sleeping." The old witch pointed a crooked finger towards Reynauld. "Now is your time to strike, for the king's body is inside near the door. The casket is heavy, and you must use your best men to carry it away."

Reynauld listened to his sage's advice and signaled his men to ready themselves. They all wore dark clothing and used only the light from the full moon to guide the group to the inn. Their mission was to kidnap the king's body. Once they had the dead king's body in a secure location, the men would shred the royal garments and pull the dead skin to the bare bones. After the bones had time to dry, the dark knights would break each piece of the body to form single sections, and then the process of grinding them to dust would begin. Revenge was, indeed, a very powerful intoxicant when a lost honor was at stake and to be reclaimed in triumph.

In three-quarters of an hour, Reynauld's men were in position surrounding the tavern. The men had a wagon and a team of four horses nearby, prepared to haul away their prize. The old witch had been correct. The guards were asleep, and the casket was inside unattended and close to the front door.

Two of the attackers crept forward in the cover of darkness and bludgeoned the two English guards asleep at the fire pit outside. Other assailants swept past the fallen men and entered the establishment. The entire tavern was silent except for the dying fire in the main hearth. Small crackles and pops could be heard from the smoldering embers which were once the roaring fire that had warmed the entire dining area.

It took eight men to lift the heavy casket. The Frenchmen became excited as the plan unfolded before them. Protests of the immense weight of the casket were beginning to be whispered as the dead king's body shifted inside the casket. A putrid odor emanated from within the lead-lined box. The eight stout men struggled to keep control of their heavy treasure.

Suddenly, one of the men began to show signs of nausea. His arms locked in a deadly tug of war with the heavy box. He couldn't let go, yet the foul smell invaded his nostrils like wisps of death. The man was clearly in misery as he was one of the last men at the end of the casket. His right hand began to feel something strange. An ooze of greenish slime poured out of the corner of the large casket and covered the man's hand. He looked down to see the vile liquid pouring out and dripping to the floor. The smells of such a horrible liquid finally did the poor fellow in, and he fainted.

The other seven men quickly compensated for the added weight and responsibility. The soldier who had passed out was left behind inside the tavern. The tavern owner's dog, who had been asleep the entire time, began to rouse to see what was going on. The canine trotted over to the wet green spots of slime on the floor and licked the goo up.

The seven large men hurried across the open ground to the nearby wagon and its two additional men. Once there, they quickly hoisted the king's remains into the back as the two drivers struggled to keep the team in check. The box still leaking a foul fluid. The wagon team neighed and snorted at their cargo's stench. One horse whinnied louder than the others in protest.

"Halt, in the name of the king! Who goes there?" asked a voice from the corner of the tavern.

Four of the king's vergers, who had made camp near the woods away from the inn, came out from the shadows. Each verger wore the tunic of their dead king. Each was armed with a war mace of hardened wood and iron spikes, a heavy armored club to some but a nightmare of pain and death to others who had seen its lethality on the field of battle.

The French knights and men-at-arms were caught completely by surprise. They were not prepared for battle. Their swords were on the cart. Some of the weapons were trapped underneath the heavy casket, and most were covered in the vile ooze. The wagon team took off in the confusion with the two drivers whipping the horses into a full gallop.

Only one Frenchman had a bow, and he fired off two arrows in quick succession, killing one verger and wounding another. The other vergers charged into the Frenchmen and shouted alarms to the guards inside the tavern to awaken and help save the king.

Shouts and calls to action began to come from inside the tavern, both upstairs and downstairs. More Englishmen joined the fray and assisted their verger brethren. The French soldiers were quickly outnumbered and started to worry about their chances to live out the night.

A great cloud of dark gray smoke appeared in the middle of the melee. Every combatant was instantly frozen in time. Some soldiers were even in mid-strike with their weapon, yet they could not move.

Cassandra revealed herself from the smoke and looked around her to ensure that everyone was affected by the spell. Her gray cloak seemed almost spectral when blended with the smoke. To some observer looking from a short distance, Cassandra seemed to be only a head surrounded by a dark and billowy cloud.

She used her staff and touched the remaining Frenchmen. This action freed the soldiers from the spell, and she instructed them to leave quickly, an order they promptly obeyed.

Looking around to see if she had done her duty, she smiled and morphed her frail human form into the black crow that she was most familiar with and flew away. Cawing with each flap of her wings as if teasing the Englishmen, she climbed higher and higher into the air. Her crow feet clutched a small wooden stick which was her staff while in human form. It was from within that staff that Cassandra drew her strength and power. When she became a crow or a raven, the staff changed with her.

Back at the inn, everyone was coming to from the spell. As the last of the soldiers were regaining control of their bodies, a brown-haired verger came rushing towards the soldiers who had been engaged in battle as he finished buttoning up his coat.

"What happened?" asked Paul Cotter, captain of the vergers. He surveyed the scene as his rough hand rubbed the jagged scar from a long-ago battle that marred the right side of his neck.

"Thieves, marauders, enemies of the state… I don't know!" a red-faced verger cried out, not caring if he was being insolent. He pointed at the soldiers emerging in a stupor from the inn. "All I know is that while those bastards were wenching and drinking until they all passed out, they gave no thought to the safety of the king's body."

From the door of the tavern, a black-haired guard called to Cotter. "Captain Cotter, one of them is still alive! Look here, inside the tavern. He's starting to come to."

Captain Cotter knew that the king's men were in very deep trouble. One, their charge of protecting the king's body was a failure. Two, the verger was right: the entire group had been derelict and drunk on duty. If word got out about the kidnapping, their heads would roll as punishment. He knew he had to take charge and do it quickly.

"Here," commanded Captain Cotter as he turned and headed towards the door of the inn. He waved a hand in the air. "Grab that buffoon and let's start waking him up and see if he wants to talk or die."

CHAPTER 14: FISH, CRABS, AND OTHER THINGS

England, 1547

Reynauld and his guild were quick to make it back to their camp along the river. There were plenty of trees and heavy underbrush to conceal their activities. One of his men drove the team of horses and wagon back to where they had stolen them. The soldier had been instructed to leave the wagon hitched and a coin in the driver's seat as compensation.

The rest of the men were instructed not to start any fires and to eat the rest of the salted meat and stale bread. A bottle of rancid wine was passed around to everyone's displeasure. There were grumblings among the knights about what was to happen next, as the situation seemed bleak.

As his knights ate, Reynauld paced along the water's edge, lost in thought about what to do about the king's corpse. The smell was beyond any tolerance and would give the group away if they were being tracked by hounds. They couldn't burn the king's body to rid it of its clothing soiled with a blackish goo and its putrid flesh that had already turned black. A fire and its rising smoke would only tip off the king's trackers as to their location. Perplexed to a standstill, Reynauld stopped pacing and called out for help. "Cassandra?"

"Yes, my lord?" came a whisper from the air.

Reynauld looked around for some sign of the witch. "What am I to do with your friend here?"

From behind Reynauld, as if hiding in his shadow, Cassandra appeared. Reynauld's men shuddered by her sudden appearance. Reynauld turned to face the withered old woman.

"Take the king's clothing and attach a large boulder to the bundle and throw it into the river. Put the lead casket over there underneath the brush." She pointed to the brush and then toward a spot further down the riverbank. "Down the river at the first bend are some fishermen's nets. Retrieve them and wrap the king's body in the nets. Weigh the body down with large rocks and put him into the water at the deep end. Make sure the body is secure. The fish and fresh water crabs will eat his bones clean. Then you can begin your grisly revenge of grinding his bones."

Reynauld looked to his lieutenants and nodded his head, turning the witch's suggestion into an order. He ran his hand across his pale, haggard face and let out a deep breath as his men rose and set to work stripping the putrid body.

"Ten paces from that rocky bank, there," Reynauld counseled his men when they had attached the clothes to a large boulder and secured the body in the nets. He pointed to the place in the river. "Anchor the body there. Excellent!"

The king's body and clothing were interred in the cold dark waters of the river. Its lazy currents swallowed up the nets and its cargo like a dark shadow covering a flower.

A moment of silence embraced Reynauld's men. Cassandra seemed to be pleased that her grand plan of her ways returning was working. A fresh breeze blew through the trees that finally rid the men of the awful smell of death. Only a series of small bubbles rose up from the murky depth that marked the king's position. It was a good omen to them.

Reynauld turned to the witch who stood near the trees, his dark eyes glazed with the vengeance and hatred that consumed his heart. "How long will this take, Cassandra?"

"In the state his body was in, it will only take a day," she replied with a wicked grin. "I suggest you disperse your men and have them bathe. Then they can return and carry on with the mission. The night will be dark, and a storm will conceal your actions in recovering the nets and bones."

Cassandra walked over to the river and started a new incantation with her staff. She twirled the walking stick several times in the river. Instantly, a large number of fish and crabs appeared. These aquatic riverkeepers dove beneath the surface and began to consume the king's rotting flesh and sinew. Like a bubbling brook, the location of the submerged nets brought up a tempest of activity as the fish and crabs devoured their prize.

"It won't take long," she whispered, knowing her spell would continue through the night.

CHAPTER 15: IF A PIECE OF WOOD COULD TALK

England, 1547

A large wooden pail that sat on the heavy wooden table was filled to the rim with water from a nearby well. The king's men stood around the large table inside the tavern facing the only man seated in a chair at the table. He was in a haggard state, as if tossed around on the cold stone floor one too many times by his captors. It was the afternoon after the attack, and despite the seemingly endless hours of interrogation, the king's men still couldn't beat the information out of their prisoner.

A brown burlap sack once used to carry oats was placed over the man's head. He was silent with his hooded head bent in submission and his arms tied behind his back. The pail of water was moved closer to the edge of the table by a soldier.

Through the stitches of the burlap bag, the captive viewed what was on the table, and he began to smile. He hoped that, perhaps, he was finally going to get a drink of some fresh water. Perhaps, he could wash off that foul green slime from the dead king's casket, then dried and attached to his skin in places like splattered mud. He had told his captors everything he wanted them to know... except for one thing. He knew he could never tell that secret, or he would surely die a most painful death. Somehow, he had to survive or die by his enemy's hand or, worse, his own.

The English guards and vergers closed ranks around the table and pulled the sack slowly off the Frenchman's head. It was at that very moment that the prisoner knew he wasn't going to get that drink of water, and he began to squirm. The king's men pounced and grabbed the French prisoner like a bowl of sardines placed in the middle of ten hungry cats and promptly forced his face into the bucket of water. Water splashed everywhere as the victim's head was submerged.

"Ah, he's holdin' his breath, sir," grumbled one of the soldiers.

Captain Cotter walked behind the prisoner and kicked the old chair out from under the man, sending the man reeling as the soldiers held his head and the bucket firmly in place. This action scared the Frenchman into screaming into the water around his head as his throat met with the upper part of the bucket before the soldiers caught him by the rope tying his arms together to keep him from pulling the bucket off the table with him and onto the floor. Unable to lift his head and losing valuable air, it was only a matter of time before the Frenchman fell limp, supported only by the soldiers around him.

"Bring him up," ordered Captain Cotter, motioning with his hand.

The man's face was lifted only a few inches from the bucket, and he gasped and choked for air. He stood there, bent over, surrounded by soldiers, his legs wobbling and still too weak to keep him up on his own. He was scared, for the strength of his will quickly vanished when he couldn't breathe. He knew it was only a minute before they would dunk his face again. He had to think fast as to what to do. He licked his lips for some life-giving water even though seconds before it had been the very same water that was to take his life away.

Captain Cotter snarled as he watched the man lick his lips. "Again!"

"No, wait!" The Frenchman shook his head and coughed. "I will tell you what you want to know."

"Not good enough," Cotter replied sternly. "Offer him another taste."

Again, the men forced the Frenchman's head into the water. It was for just a short time, but it was enough to convince the Frenchman that it was his last chance. When he was brought up again, he sounded more convincing, like a man who had just died and was walking towards an uncertain future only to be offered the door to life and the mortal world he so enjoyed. A brown-haired verger retrieved the chair and slid it in behind the Frenchman as the soldiers sat him down.

The Frenchman coughed, water spewing from his lips. He looked at Cotter with hatred in his eyes. "Your dead king murdered our knights and soldiers at the Battle of the Black Flags. You English pigs butchered my father and his brother. There are stories that the French army had even surrendered, yet you still killed the lot of our host."

Cotter moved to the edge of the table, looming above his prisoner. "Where did your fellows take our king?"

"There is a clearing at the river bank where there are some boulders that jut out into the water. That is our camp." The Frenchman again licked his lips, glaring up at Cotter. "However, they surely will be gone by now."

The red-faced verger nodded and said, "Captain, Frenchie means the place called Nag's Head on the river."

"Gather the horses!" Cotter ordered. "We ride to this place immediately. If we hurry, we should get there by dusk."

The knights, guards, and vergers quickly scattered and began to make preparations for the chase. The innkeeper was charged with keeping the Frenchman prisoner and giving him some food and water. A silver coin was cheaper than losing a man to guard a worthless prisoner.

The sound of swords in scabbards, chainmail, leather clothing, and horses soon choked the quiet afternoon of the day.

Unknown to the king's men, a curious old crow had been watching from the branch of the old oak tree that shaded half of the tavern. Through the open tavern front door and windows, the crow had seen and heard everything the men had inflicted on the prisoner. She watched through the window as the prisoner was given some food and water by the innkeeper while the soldiers hurried about. From her perch, she then watched as the horsemen rode away west on the county road. When they were out of sight, the crow flew down to the ground and waved one its claws that held tightly to a small stick. In an instant, Cassandra appeared, unseen by the people inside the tavern. She then hobbled forward, using her staff as an old peasant woman would, and entered the tavern.

"Hello, dear," she said in a wispy voice as she shuffled towards the table the innkeeper was wiping off a table.

The innkeeper nodded in greeting. "What can we offer you today? We have potato and onion soup with a bit of old beef for two coins. Three coins gets you bread and some ale if you like."

Cassandra continued with her act and sat down at the very same table where the French prisoner had been tortured. Her hands moved over the wood as if she could hear the old wooden table tell her the story of pain and water. The table even spoke to her about a time when some foolish human had carved his initials into its side, causing so much pain and scars. Her crippled old fingers tapped gently on the table as if she acknowledged the table's suffering and thanked it for revealing what had transpired.

Cassandra looked around the quiet room and saw someone taking the wet and battered prisoner with his hands tied behind him into the back area where there was a root cellar below the tavern for storing goods. She made a mental note of what needed to be done and turned back to the innkeeper.

"Nothing for me, good fellow. I'm too old for good food. That ale you mentioned sounds tempting, though. Might I have a taste of it before I buy?"

"Now look here! I'll give you a taste, but there will be no begging here, you understand?" responded the keeper, a slight snarl replacing the smile from before.

He marched across the room and took a flagon from his bar area and opened the cask for a quick dribble of the ale. He walked slowly over to the older woman. He was sure he had seen her before, but he tried vainly to remember where. He placed the pewter flagon on the table. His hand was letting go of the handle when Cassandra's hand grabbed it with such speed and skill it startled him. He tried to react by pulling his hand away, but Cassandra had already begun her trap as a spell quickly wrapped around the man's head with confusion and a touch of obedience.

"Now, bring me my soup and bread," she whispered, staring into the frozen man's eyes. "I want the nice bread you have hidden underneath in that cabinet over there. I punished you last time you tried to cheat me, so you remember that."

"Yes, ma'am," the tavern owner softly said. He was totally in a trance as Cassandra's magic controlled her prey, and he hurried off to retrieve her soup and bread.

After Cassandra had her fill, she slowly rose from the table and went to the back of the tavern to the root cellar door. It was not locked, and as she pushed open the heavy wooden door, the musty smell of the cold, damp earth awaiting her at the bottom of the dirt steps filled her nostrils. She inhaled deeply, a small smile stretching her thin withered lips ominously as she recognized the smell of fear mingled with the earthen musk. She slowly stepped forward and slowly descended the dirt steps into the darkness below.

Several yards away, stray beams of light from the openings in the floor above danced with the shadows on the prisoner. He was blindfolded and tied up to a post that supported the floor above. Sweat glistened on his brow as he nervously moved his head from side-to side from the instinctual need to see who had come downstairs to see him. The blindfold was not like the burlap sack, and his efforts were in vain. In the still and quiet darkness, he was totally alone and frightened, each noise in the earthen room amplified by his fear.

"Who... who's there?" he asked, his voice trembling.

Cassandra said nothing. She only reached into an old leather pouch that was attached with some string to a roughshod belt of dried deer skin around her waist. She pulled out a handful of seeds and poured some into the palm of her left hand. The seeds had white tails with a brown husked shell. The chalky white tails stood up straight and moved slowly back and forth like a long-tailed cat spying a lovely mouse in the corner. She was very careful not to let any of the seeds blow off her fingers as she quietly approached the man. Each rustle of her dress and careful footstep echoed like thunder in the prisoner's ears.

"Who's there?" he asked again, the fear welling inside him causing his voice to rise. "Is it...? I... I... I didn't say a thing. I... I didn't."

He began to squirm again with his head moving back and forth against the post in the attempt to try to move the blindfold so he could see. He knew someone or something was moving closer to him as each soft step sent amplified his fear. He felt a chill run through him like an early spring morning with a touch of winter's kiss that was still in the air. Goose pimples formed quickly and stood out on the man's skin.

"I... I ... I swear...!" he called out between deep inhales. Panic welled inside of him, making each breath harder to take. "I swear I didn't say a word!"

His mouth was held open as he gasped for breath, the fear within him squeezing his lungs. Cassandra held up her hand and quickly blew the white-tailed seeds into the man's gaping mouth. The man gagged and tried to spit the seeds out, but he needed to breathe and it only forced the seeds deeper into his lungs.

In an instant, he felt extremely tired. He could feel his life draining away like the sand in a glass timepiece.

"I swear...," he choked out between coughs and gags. His voice weakened as if the last bit of air was being squeezed from his lungs. "I... didn't... tell... them."

His words turned to moans as his muscles turned into long straight ridges; his skin began to dry and change into a pale bark. His torso stiffened and changed form into the trunk of some grotesque tree. He was dying as a human, yet he was changing into something else, new and alive, incredibly fast.

Sounds of creaking, moaning, and breaking could be heard emanating from his body as he gasped for air, still choking on the white-tailed seeds. His feet sprouted roots that sunk deeply into the clay floor of the root cellar searching for water underneath the soil. Other roots moved and slithered just underneath the earth. His arms grew upwards, breaking the ropes that bound him to the support post. Hands turning into branches, fingers piercing the outer wall of the tavern seeking sunlight as Cassandra's unique tree grew. Planks of siding broke free and allowed sunlight into the once-dark cellar. Camel crickets and centipedes quickly scampered away to find the comfort of darkness once again.

The blindfold finally fell away, exposing the man's then withered face as terrified eyes dried up to become part of the tree as well. The man was no longer a man; he was a living tree trapped eternally by his feet in the dirt and his hands through the floor and out the side of the building. He was no more.

The low moans he had made as a mortal man were then masked by the bark that had grown over his lips and nostrils. By that point, the sounds of a true tree moaning could be heard as if the tree were in a gentle wind moving its branches in a forest and talking to its kin in a wood. A similar tree across the road moaned a response and gently waved its branches back and forth, evidence of Cassandra's earlier handicraft with white-tailed seeds ages before.

Cassandra quietly turned herself into her crow shape. She gathered the tiny stick that was her staff in her mouth and hopped up onto one of the newly made tree branches and walked up through the opening that the arms had made. Once outside, she flew towards the gathering place where the English were riding to save their dead king's body.

CHAPTER 16: ESSEX AND CHELMSFORD CATHEDRAL

England, 2014

Michael woke with a start, sweat streaming down his face and onto his neck. He glanced around the room, taking in his surroundings as he sat up and let out a deep breath. He squeezed his eyes shut, and visions of Rachel's lifeless body flashed in his mind. Michael jerked his eyes open again then inhaled deeply and let out another long breath. It had been a long, restless night filled with dreams about David's dying words and Rachel's murder the night before. Even though he was awake, the images still whirled in his mind as the guilty feeling that it could have been him both times gripped his heart.

He shook his head, trying to clear his thoughts, and a sharp pain emanated from the right side of his neck. He instinctively reached up to the bandage there. It was soaking wet. He looked down at his hand as he pulled it away, and his fingers were damp with blood. He wiped his hand on his t-shirt and got off the couch. He grabbed his bag and headed down the hall of Tommy's apartment to the bathroom to clean his wound and get dressed. The need to be done with his mission was great, and he knew that the sooner it was over, the sooner he would have some peace about David's death.

In the bathroom, Michael uncovered his wound and applied some pressure with a new gauze. It was barely bleeding, so he knew that most of what had caused the dampness was his own sweat. He redressed the wound, washed his face, and brushed his teeth before getting dressed. As he opened the bathroom door and stepped into the hall, the door to Bernard's room opened a crack.

"Hey. What are you doing up so early?" Bernard whispered sleepily, peering through the slightly opened door.

Michael smiled weakly. "Go back to sleep. I have to do something."

Bernard smiled back and nodded before shutting the door. Michael walked down the hall and tossed his bag on the floor next to the couch. He retrieved the small wooden box from beneath the pillow and stuffed it in his pocket before straightening up where he'd slept. As he put away the hide-a-bed, Bernard was down the hall quickly getting dressed behind his closed door.

Once Michael was finished, he left, quietly closing the apartment door behind him. As soon as Bernard heard the door close, he opened his door and hurried down the hallway. He glanced around the tidied-up room before he hurried to the door to follow Michael. He quickly dialed a number on his cellphone as he quietly closed the apartment door behind him so as not to wake Tommy.

A light railway station was two blocks from Tommy's apartment, and Michael purchased a roundtrip ticket there to Chelmsford in Essex. While he waited for his train to arrive, he grabbed a quick bite at the small deli just outside the station. It was 9:16 a.m., and the train was early for some reason. He quickly gobbled down his egg biscuit, wadding up the foil paper wrapper and lobbing the trash into a garbage bin. The cup of coffee he'd bought was horrible, but it was hot and felt good going down.

"Mental note, Michael: order hot tea next time," he whispered under his breath.

A station attendant waved a finger to Michael that his hot drink had to be disposed of in the trash. Michael took one last gulp and tossed the cup into the bin as well.

"Mind the gap, please," sounded an automated voice from the train car.

Michael hurried forward and climbed into the fourth car from the front engine, the first car in second class. His destination was 40 miles away, a 57-minute ride by car, but for Michael, a train ride was a great way to get away from it all for a day. The train was scheduled to make several stops before the station in Chelmsford, so he hoped he would have time for a quick nap. He found a seat near the back of the car and settled in, his eyelids heavy from the restless night before.

"Ticket, please," said the conductor.

Michael blinked and looked up. "Hmmm? Sorry, I dozed off."

The tall man stood above Michael with his hand out. "Ticket, please."

"Are we in the Essex area yet? I am on my way to Chelmsford to see the cathedral there," said Michael as he handed his ticket to the conductor.

The train employee had a baffled look on his face, clicked his ticket and handed it back to him. "We will get there in about half an hour. Are you American?"

"Yes, sir," Michael said, nodding, "on vacation."

"Chelmsford Cathedral is lovely this time of spring. The trees have fully bloomed. Be sure to visit some of the other places, like the several museums, parks, and art centers. I'll come back this way and give you a nudge to wake you, son." With that, the conductor moved to the next car.

Michael thanked the conductor dozed off again. His cellphone rang, waking him.

"Michael? It's me, where are you?" his cousin Elizabeth asked. "I'm here at Heathrow with Steven. We landed about an hour ago and are waiting for you!"

Michael had totally lost all track of time with the shooting at the pub and staying over with Bernard and Tommy at his place.

"Oh, shit! Elizabeth! I am so sorry. I had an emergency and had to take care of this first thing this morning. Where are you guys staying? I'm on my way to Chelmsford, Essex, and will not be back until around six this evening."

Michael heard her say something and fumbling on the other end of the line.

"Hey, brother, it's me," Steve said. "It's okay. Elizabeth and I will head over to our hotel. Mom and Dad fixed us up at the Landmark in downtown London. We have reservations for room 316."

"Thanks, Steve," Michael said. He let out a sigh of relief. He was glad his younger brother was so thoughtful. "I really am sorry. My train will be back around six."

"There is a train station just outside the side entrance to the hotel from what I read online. I also saw there is a pizza restaurant just across the street from the hotel, half a block down on the right. See you there at 7:00. You can buy us dinner to make up."

"Sure thing," Michael replied. He could hear Steve laughing as he returned Elizabeth's cellphone to her.

"I wanted to meet Michael's friends," cried Elizabeth in the background before the line went dead.

The thought of catching another nap had totally vaporized with the adrenaline rush of making such a clumsy mistake. Michael knew he had to get his act together before he arrived at the cathedral. To reassure himself, he patted his pants' pocket and felt the box in there.

As promised, not much later, the train conductor walked by Michael's seat and nodded gently to the American that this was, indeed, his stop. Michael smiled back and quietly looked out the train window. In the distance, he could barely see the green patina spire of the cathedral past the trees.

From the train station, Michael took a cab ride to the church. He used his phone and researched a quick history of the church online on the cab ride over. Officially known as the Cathedral Church of St. Mary the Virgin, it had been built over 800 years before between the years of 1200 and 1520 AD. The church had been extended in the early 1950s to honor the brave American airmen stationed in the Essex area during World War II. That part was of particular interest to Michael due to his relationship with the military. The online article also said that Henry VIII was fond of that cathedral during its construction. The king had passed away in 1547 AD.

The cab pulled up in front of the church, and Michael paid the cabbie before heading to the door of the church as the cab drove away. The front entrance was locked. The massive cathedral doors reminded Michael of some grand fortress. Looking around to try to determine what he should do next, Michael noted a small placard posted that informed visitors to proceed to the side entrance to the right. He walked around the side to find that door was locked as well. There was an intercom box mounted next to the door. He pressed the button.

A few seconds later, a voice responded, "Who is there?"

"Michael Cotter. I need to meet with the head verger, a man named Lark."

There was no response for a long time. Michael thought he had possibly pushed the button wrong and hadn't transmitted his message. After what seemed like ages passed, the side door opened. Michael was relieved to finally meet someone.

A small older man appeared in the doorway. He smiled kindly. "We apologize for the doors being locked. We have had way too many transients come through our small city, and we had to take precautions due to vagrants stealing our property."

"I understand." Michael smiled back at the man and nodded in understanding. "Please, I need to meet the verger named Lark. Is he here?"

"Yes," the old man answered, stepping aside to let Michael enter. "This way, please."

CHAPTER 17: HELLO, EVIL, WE HAVE MET BEFORE

England, 2014

Michael followed the old man through the nave. They both paused in front of the main altar where they genuflected by bending a right knee to show respect to Christ. After a short pause, they rose, and the old man led the way into a narrow hallway.

"Are you Anglican, sir?" asked the attendant, glancing at Michael over his shoulder.

"Well, yes. I'm American, and I'm Episcopalian, which I guess is the same as Anglican."

"Sorry? Oh, yes, that is confusing. We all think we are a part of the Church of England. It's amazing what a little revolution can create," the old man replied in a haughty tone.

Michael gave a sideways smile, slightly uncomfortable with the man's tone. They came to a place where the narrow hallway met another hallway. The old man stopped and turned to face Michael.

"Here we are," he said, raising a hand to point the way. "Second door to the left. Please knock before you enter. He had a meeting earlier with some guests from France. I believe they are finished, though."

"Thank you." Michael nodded and started around the corner.

"Don't forget to knock. Good day to you," the old man said and then disappeared back down the narrow hallway.

Michael began to feel a bit nervous, even though he knew it was the final phase in David's dying wish to get the box in his pocket back to the church.

"Why to Lark? Who was he to David?" Michael whispered to himself as he walked down the hallway. He stopped in front of the door the old man had indicated. "Well, here we go."

Michael tapped twice on the wooden office door.

"Enter," came a voice from inside.

Michael opened the door only to be surprised at the small size of that office. He had expected some large room filled with volumes of historical data, perhaps, even a large desk and a stained glass window. Instead, Michael found the room to be very cramped. Its occupant, the verger, was a small man with poor posture. He wore a black cassock like a priest would wear, but it was without the white tab at the neck.

The gaunt man sat at his desk, elbows touching the red velvet padding on the arm rests of the chair. His hands were clasped and poised in front of his aged and wrinkled face. A pair of half-rimmed reading glasses perched on the bridge of his pointed nose. To Michael, Lark was the image of an old crow. Sitting in his chair, the verger looked at Michael as if sizing him up for a meal, or worse.

"Mr. Lark, I presume?" Michael asked as he peered into the room. "I am Lieutenant Michael Cotter of the United States Army. I was posted with a British artillery unit in Afghanistan. My best friend, David Brown, was a verger for you here at the cathedral."

"Ah, yes," the old man said, nodding. He motioned Michael forward with his thin, bony finger. "Come in. Come in, please, lieutenant. Have a seat. Are you here on holiday? We do not get many visitors in the spring. Tell me, where are you staying? Close by, I hope?"

Michael entered the room, shutting the door behind him. "I am staying with some friends in a flat in downtown London. We all used to work together at a company called BADS. Electronics and the sort."

Lark motioned for Michael to come closer with his bony finger, smiling encouragingly.

"I can only stay a little while," Michael said, taking another step forward. "I need to take the 4:20 afternoon train back to London. My sister and brother are flying in from the States, and we are to meet at the Landmark Hotel later today."

Michael paused for a brief moment. He still was standing and had perplexed himself as to why he had to give all of that personal information to a complete stranger. He thought it must be his nerves. He couldn't help but also think that Mr. Lark surely had better things to do than listen to him. At the same time, he felt like his rambling might be some ill omen about the man before him. Michael shrugged off his nervous jitters and gathered his courage to tell the old verger the bad news about David.

"Was?" Lark asked.

Michael shook his head, refocusing on the man before him. "Excuse me?"

"You said David... was." The old verger's head tilted slightly to the right and then straightened.

"Yes, sir." Michael looked down for a moment and took a deep breath before returning his gaze to the man behind the desk. "David was killed in action."

Lark brought down his hands in disbelief. He paused for several minutes, and then he reached over and picked up his cellphone and pressed a speed dial button. He then quietly summoned someone to his office. He pressed a button to end the call and laid the phone on his desk.

"Please, have a seat there," Lark said as he motioned for Michael to take a seat. "There is someone else who I know will want to hear this news."

The two waited briefly and then a knock came at the door.

"Please enter," Lark called out.

A tall, bulking man with dark hair entered the room. His shoulders were almost as wide as the doorway, and the long black cassock he wore was stretched across his gargantuan frame to the point that is looked as if it might rip at any moment.

"Please close the door behind you," Lark said, nodding at the man as he closed the door and stood in front of it with his massive arms crossed in front of his chest. "This American soldier just told me that our Brown is dead."

The enormous man stood quietly, making no response to the tragic news.

"You have come all this way to tell us this bad news?" asked Lark as he shuffled some papers on his desk.

Michael watched the old verger's knees lift and fall as if he was adjusting something on the floor under the desk. Even though Michael knew there could be some sort of footstool beneath the desk, the man's strange actions made him even more uncomfortable than he already was.

"No, sir," Michael said, hesitating. "He took something from this church for good luck and wanted it returned to you. He said that while he died in my arms, sir."

Lark's head again tilted to the side as a smile seemed to tug at the corners of his mouth before fading away. He clasped his hands together in front of him again. "Well, let's have a look at this mystery object."

Michael instantly felt strange about his conversation of David's condition with the man before him. He couldn't shake the feeling that David's friend should have been more focused on David's death than some mystery object. Also annoying was the quiet giant standing behind Michael. Avoiding eye contact, the enormous man stood there as if to bar the door from opening.

Suddenly, Michael felt as if, perhaps, he has failed his friend's wish. He inhaled deeply and let out a long sigh. Reluctantly, Michael retrieved the small wooden box from his pants' pocket and handed it over to Lark.

Lark's talon-like fingers reached out to grasp the box. Michael paused for a brief second, reflecting, then handed the box to Lark, who eagerly snatched it away.

The head verger was very still for a moment, staring down at the ornate wooden cube in his hand. He opened the box very slowly as if savoring what was before him. The large man behind Michael peered over Michael's head to see what was inside.

Lark let out a faint gasp of surprise and relish as the box opened, exposing a dull, brownish digit of a finger. Petrified and old-looking, it seemed to be a relic of some importance to Lark and his silent compatriot.

"What is it?" asked Michael.

The old verger pursed his lips as he laid the bone down on some papers on his desk. It looked strange all by itself, a dark brown stick-like object that had obviously been stored in the small container for a very long time. The finger bone looked like an anachronism from another age.

"This? This, you ask?" Lark said, tilting his head from side to side as he inspected the object before him through the half-rimmed glasses perched on the end of his nose. He shook his head. "This is nothing more than a silly old prank our David played on you. It is merely a dried-up chicken wing bone, probably from some dreary pub you fellows enjoyed in the army. You Yanks love eating those things, chicken wings, I believe."

Michael straightened in his chair, the feeling of uneasiness welling up inside him. "They are called 'buffalo wings.' And I do not believe that David, who served under you, would do such a thing with his dying breath. With all respect, sir, I don't believe you."

Lark paused for a moment as if thinking. His cold dark eyes looked up to his associate standing behind Michael, and with a scowl, Lark shook his head.

A quiet and uneasy pause crept over the room as the unknown actions of the quiet giant behind Michael unnerved him.

Lark reached over to a bookshelf to his left and picked up a rubber object on the third shelf and held the toy in front of Michael's face. It was a rubber replica of brown dog poop.

"You see that? That is what your David left for me just outside my office on one very warm and humid day. I stepped on it and almost had a heart attack thinking the worse." Lark put the fake poop back on his shelf and shook his head. "Your David was indeed a good man, soldier, verger, and friend, but he loved his pranks more than just about anything. This was his last attempt to get under my skin, at your expense I'm afraid."

Lark coldly tossed the bone and the empty box into the nearby trash bin beside his desk as Michael watched in disbelief.

"Good day to you, Lt. Cotter," Lark said as he motioned to his associate to open the door. "Thank you for your visit, but we must be going now."

Lark turned in his chair and stood. He came around the desk and outstretched his hand. Michael stood and shook the man's fragile, bony hand before turning to the door. The enormous man stepped outside the office and waited for Michael and Lark to exit. As they walked out of the office, Michael paused. "I'm sorry. I don't want to bother you, but which way is the men's restroom?"

Lark pointed down the hall. "Right down there. We must be going. We have another meeting we need to attend to."

Lark and his associate went the opposite direction to attend their meeting in another part of the cathedral as Michael made his way to the restroom down the hall. The two men rounded the corner into the narrow hallway, and Lark glanced to his companion beside him.

"We will wait out back for Lt. Cotter to leave before we return to the office. Call Vonyou and tell him that his missed target has brought us the prize we have been seeking." A gruesome smile spread across Lark's thin lips. "It is now within our midst."

After Michael relieved himself, he went over to wash his hands. He looked into the mirror above the wash basin and stared at himself in disbelief. He knew in his heart that David would not have made the box out to be so secret if it was just a practical joke. He searched for an answer, and then he remembered David's words.

"Trust no one."

Michael left the men's room and went back to Lark's office. The door was open, and the gentlemen were nowhere to be found. He knew that something was off about Lark and the other man, but he couldn't quite see what it was.

Feeling cheated of an honor for his lost friend, Michael walked into the office quickly and retrieved the bone and the box from the trash can. A piece of wadded up paper had affixed itself to the box and fell behind the desk as he pulled the box from the trash can. Michael moved forward to pick up the paper and suddenly saw a lifeless face and hand underneath the desk. When he peered around the corner of the desk, he saw a curled-up dead man in his underwear. Michael realized instantly that David's warning had, indeed, been true.

Nervous that he might have stumbled into something very dangerous, Michael felt frozen for what seemed like an eternity but, in reality, was only a few seconds. He placed the finger bone into the box and shoved it into his pants' pocket as he made for the exit. He was outside the cathedral within a few minutes.

"I've got to get away from here! Who are those priests? Why would they kill someone and try to impersonate Lark?" Michael whispered to himself as he ran down the street away from the cathedral. "Oh, David, what should I do?"

CHAPTER 18: THE BACK OF THE BUS HAS THE BEST SEATS

England, 2014

A group of pilgrimage followers were embarking a tour bus at the street corner at the end of the block the cathedral was on. The group of seniors were from Indiana and were destined to head back to London after their excursion. Michael slowed his pace and walked casually up to the group, slipping unnoticed into the crowd. He noticed that the short, blonde-haired female tour director was distracted by the bus driver who was complaining that he didn't have time to drive the group to an extra location before London.

Michael looked back and forth nonchalantly. Deciding that no one was looking at him, he climbed aboard the bus as the group of tourists moved forward. There were plenty of seats available in the rear of the bus. This was made possible because the sole lavatory on the bus had a malfunctioning pump. The stench from the full holding tank wafted through the rear end of the bus, so nobody dared to sit in the rear. For Michael, it reminded him of the full latrine barrels on the base in Afghanistan. A few riders noticed their new passenger as he made his way past them to the last seat and sat down, but they paid him no mind since he was sitting in the back.

Inside the cathedral, the Lark imposter and his gargantuan associate returned to Lark's office. As the enormous man quietly closed the door behind them, the crow-faced imposter picked up the trashcan and searched through the wadded papers and trash. His searching picked up in pace when he couldn't find the bone or the box.

"Where is it? It has to be in here. *Je suis en colere!*" cried the angry imposter as he realized Michael must have snuck back into the office and stolen the artifact.

He threw the trashcan down in disgust, spilling its contents. He clenched his talon-like fingers as he trembled with anger. "Call Vonyou and tell him that I want to have a conference with him. We have another job for him—to find and kill that American and get me back that bone!"

As the enormous man pulled out his cellphone and began to dial, the crow-faced imposter stormed past him and out the door, beckoning for his associate to follow. They picked up their pace to a slow trot as they ran to the parking lot.

Once outside, the imposter felt for a set of keys in the cassock's pocket. He pulled out the keys and pressed the "unlock" feature on the key fob. A small sedan's parking lights flashed twice, revealing its position in the parking lot. The imposter's plan was simple enough: they would take Lark's black Citroen and drive to the train station before the American headed back to London.

On the tour bus, all the passengers had boarded, and the bus slowly set off down the street. He knew that the crow-faced imposter who must have killed Lark knew too much about him and his plans for his comfort, so taking the tour bus was his quickest and safest option for reaching his destination. He knew he could grab a taxi to reach Elizabeth and Steve once he made it to the city.

Michael took a deep breath and leaned back into the seat. He ran his hand over his hair as he thought about the two murders he had encountered since coming to London. He had no reason to believe that they were connected, but he could not shake the feeling that he seemed to be in the wrong place at the wrong time too often in the past twenty-four hours. David's last words echoed to him again: *Trust no one.*

The face of the imposter with his greedy outstretched crow-like talons reaching for the ornate box flashed in his mind. He couldn't help but regret how much he'd revealed to the deadly imposter. He quietly whispered to himself, "Okay, Crow. I don't know why you killed Lark or what to do about it right now. I just hope my meeting with you doesn't come back to bite me."

He sent Tommy a quick text message to tell him that he would be staying with Steve and Elizabeth and not to worry about him. If he stayed with them, Michael knew he could at least protect his family if Crow did happen to show up somewhere else.

The adrenaline that had been running through his system after finding Lark's body had run out. His military senses knew that he shouldn't fall asleep, but an overwhelming tiredness crept over him. Knowing it would be a bit before the next stop and that Crow and his associate had no reason to think he was on the bus, Michael gave in to the need to sleep and closed his eyes. After a few minutes of rest, Michael was disturbed by a car honking and swerving back and forth as if to pass the bus on the two-lane road. The bus driver opened his window and waited for the right time in the traffic to motion with his arm that it was okay for the black car to pass him. A few seconds later, the Citroen carrying two men that looked like priests passed the bus at a great speed with their car horn still blaring.

"Stupid bloody Frenchies and their fancy-schmancy French cars! They think they own the roads here in England." The bus driver glanced over his shoulder at the tour guide in the seat across the aisle, his cheeks turning bright red from his elevated blood pressure. "My dad fought over in France to liberate those bastards from the Germans. Now look at them. Oh, geez."

The tour guide, not wanting to offend the bus driver any more than he already was, gently nodded her head in silent agreement.

The black Citroen sped on, and then it turned very sharply at the next left. The bus continued on its merry way to London using the highway. In the back seat of the bus, Michael exhaled and closed his eyes. He hoped that would be the last he saw of Crow and his associate.

CHAPTER 19: AFTER HIM

England, 2014

Vonyou inhaled deeply on his Gauloisses as he reached into his pocket and pulled out the ringing cellphone. He pressed the button and placed the phone next to his ear as he exhaled a stream of pungent smoke. "Vonyou."

"The job is back on. You must kill the American and collect the relic," Crow's oversized associate Muzzy Bruno ordered from the other end.

"Where will I find my target, Muzzy?"

"The Landmark Hotel, last name Cotter. Some additional family members will be there to meet him. Eliminate them all if needed. Report back immediately when the job is completed."

"*Oui, monsieur*," Vonyou said, ending the call and replacing the phone in his pocket.

Vonyou walked over to the window of the room he was staying in and looked out. He took a long drag of his cigarette and let his mind reflect on the Landmark's location. He knew the hotel easily enough. It was close to Hyde Park, the place where he had killed his very first person some 23 years before.

It was supposed to have been an easy grab-the-purse-and-run job, but the woman had been carrying an unseen nail file in her other hand. When he'd snatched the purse, the knife-like file had struck Vonyou in the face. The gash had been cut deep into the cheek and had bled profusely. Enraged, he'd clobbered the woman's head in such a way she'd staggered for a brief moment and then collapsed. Vonyou's hit had struck her temple and caused a cerebral hemorrhage inside the woman's skull. She'd died before she'd hit the sidewalk.

Bleeding severely, he'd seen the hotel and had run towards the entrance. The main doorman had stopped Vonyou before he could enter the lobby.

Vonyou had tried to lie that he'd been attacked by a mugger in the park, but the doorman had only offered to call an ambulance. Vonyou had waited for a few minutes while he tried to think of way to enter the lobby. Suddenly, a policewoman had appeared and told the doorman that a woman had been found murdered in the park. The doorman and the bobby had then focused their gaze on Vonyou, who'd been smoking a cigarette and clutching a blood-stained handkerchief to his wound.

Vonyou had quickly realized that he was being observed and had bolted towards the left rear of the hotel where a subway station was close by. The bobby had blown her alert whistle and yelled for Vonyou to stop. The doorman had quickly grabbed his walkie-talkie and ordered a lockdown of the hotel for anyone trying to get in.

The intense pace of all the players had only gotten worse when Vonyou had run into an American tourist with his young daughter as they were trying to give a homeless man a heavy coat to stay warm in through the cold nights. Vonyou had run into the American and knocked down the cute little girl as well. He had then wrenched the coat away from the homeless man and had continued running while putting on the coat to change his appearance.

The American had picked himself up and helped his daughter to her feet. "Hey, you! That's my coat you stole!"

"I thought it was my coat," the transient had protested.

Vonyou caught himself touching the old scar on his cheek as he realized that he was daydreaming. He turned and walked away from the window. He took another long drag off the cigarette and crushed it out in the ashtray on his nightstand.

CHAPTER 20: KNOCK… KNOCK?

England, 2014

Elizabeth and Steve entered the extravagant hotel lobby of the Landmark, a magnificent example of dignity and grace in the modern world. The hotel staff greeted the two Americans, and after identifications were cleared, the cousins received their room key.

The attendant behind the reception desk pointed across the lobby towards the elevator. "Room 316. Take the lift, and it will be the third room to your left."

"Thank you." answered Elizabeth, brushing her shoulder-length red hair back from her face with her hand. Her blue eyes twinkled as a broad smile spread across her freckled face.

A few minutes later, Steve and Elizabeth were on their floor and proceeded to the room.

"Here it is, 316," Steve said as he tried the key in the lock. "Hey! The key won't work. The door is still locked."

He ran his hand through his short brown hair and scratched his head in confusion. Shaking his head, he tried again to get the latch to turn but with no luck. Just then, he and Elizabeth heard someone inside the room undoing the security chain and opening the door.

"Can I help you?" asked a dazed American as the other member of his family stirred from her jetlagged slumber.

"Oh, sorry. We were assigned this room," apologized Elizabeth.

A tall, slender woman in grey business suit with a gold badge on her lapel emerged from an open doorway down the hall. Seeing the confusion, she closed the door behind her and walked over.

"What's all this?" she asked, smiling cordially. "I am the floor manager. I was inspecting the rooms that have just been cleaned. Is there a problem?"

"This was supposed to be our room," Elizabeth replied politely.

In the meantime, the sleepy American had gently closed the door to 316. He shuffled back to the bed where his wife was underneath the fabulous duvet of Egyptian linen. Within moments, he was back asleep in his wife's arms.

"Well, this is a silly pickle, my dears," the floor manager said, raising her eyebrows. She reached into her pocket and pulled out another key. "Here, take this key. It's to room 307. It has just been cleaned and is ready. You two move in there, and I will take your key to reception and notify the staff at the desk of the room change. Off you go."

Elizabeth and Steve were too tired to put up any resistance and quickly followed the instructions of the supervisor. To their relief, the door opened on the first try and they entered.

Room 307 was beautiful. There were fresh-cut flowers that filled the air with a wonderful fragrance. The fine polished brass work of the sinks, shower, and bath were impeccable. The minibar was fully stocked and all free of charge as a courtesy to the guests of the Landmark.

Both Steve and Elizabeth let out a sigh of relief as they claimed the two beds for their personal domain. Steve texted Michael as to the room change. The text was sent at 5:46 p.m.

CHAPTER 21: THE SCENT OF DEATH

England, 2014

Like a veiled shadow, Vonyou slipped through the side entrance close to the subway station along with several people entering the hotel. His presence blended in with the other guests. It was his purpose as an assassin to blend in. The light brown trench coat he wore was useful should he need to make an escape by turning it inside out to the black side. The only chink in his ethereal-like armor was the stench of his nicotine habit. The other patrons noticed the smell, but they soon forgot the nasal intrusion as they went their way and Vonyou went his.

Vonyou knew his target was there, yet he did not know which room. He didn't want to go to the front desk, for it would blow his cover. There was, however, a house phone on a small side table in the lobby's hallway. It was away from prying eyes and the ever-present security cameras. He casually walked over then picked up the receiver and dialed the front desk.

"How may I help you?" came a pleasant voice from the other end.

"Ah, yes, hello," Vonyou answered. "I am looking for my niece and nephew. They are staying here with you. I have tried calling them on their cellphones, but I don't get an answer. You will find it under Cotter, Steve and Elizabeth, from America. Would you help me, please? It's kind of a family emergency."

In the background, he could hear the front desk attendant as she clicked her mouse on the hotel's registration computer. The sudden rush of new guests had temporarily overwhelmed the new hire who had just been promoted to the front desk. Vonyou could tell she was struggling, but he did hear her barely whisper, "316."

Vonyou smiled.

"One moment, sir," the attendant said into the phone. "I will connect you."

"No, what room are they in, my dear?" Vonyou persisted.

"I'm awfully sorry, sir, but I am not allowed to give you that information. It is for security reasons, you know. Shall I ring the room for you, sir?"

"No, don't bother, my dear. I will catch up with them soon enough," Vonyou said softly as he hung up the phone. "Room 316 is all I needed."

CHAPTER 22: A WAKE-UP CALL WON'T BE NEEDED

England, 2014

Vonyou rode the elevator to his target's floor. Room 316 was to the left. Within his coat pocket was a 9mm pistol with a screwed-on silencer. In his other hand was an electronic signal box that emitted a wide spectrum of signals that imitated a hotel room lock's electronic receiver frequency, a modern-day lock pick. It was a simple device he'd made using a stolen key card maker that hotel front desks use when they are assigning the credit card-shaped key for each room.

   As the elevator doors opened, he looked both ways to see if anyone was approaching then made his move. The electronic box he held found the right signal, and the door to room 316 opened easily. He entered and closed the door behind him. He could see the outline of two bodies under the covers. No one moved, for the occupants were asleep. He brought out his gun and made two head shots, killing both as they slept. The only sound was the two quiet pops as the bullets hit the white duvet that sounded like two quick strikes with a stick into a down pillow.

   Vonyou then pulled back the cover to see if anyone remained alive. Stunned, he realized there was a third person in the bed, a little girl in the middle, fast asleep. She never knew what had happed to her parents, nor would she ever. Vonyou killed her with his third shot. He then proceeded to search the room for the wooden box and finger bone that his masters wanted retrieved.

   His cellphone started to vibrate in his pants' pocket, indicating a call. He pulled it out and checked the number: it was his employer. He pressed the button to answer as he placed the phone next to his ear.

"Have you found the package?" Crow asked from the other end.

"I have eliminated the family as you demanded and have begun my search. It is here, but it must be hidden," he replied.

"We will send up the Mole to help you look. Do not fail us, Vonyou."

"I do not need that brat telling me my job. I will find the box and bring it to you. You just better have my money when I deliver the bone."

Vonyou pressed the button to end the call and stuffed the phone back into his pocket in disgust. He then searched the room for the bone and the wooden box for close to an hour. He took apart their suitcases, their bags, and even the little girl's teddy bear. The room safe wasn't closed, and there wasn't anything inside. His failed searched infuriated him. He knew that soon Mole would be knocking on the door. Vonyou didn't even know the young man's name, but he had never liked him. The boy's knowledge of technology was far superior to Vonyou's, and he knew it.

"Ahhh, there is nothing here. I need to leave and retrace my steps. Maybe I've missed something." Vonyou said as he walked out of the hotel room and proceeded to the emergency stairs.

He was careful to keep his face directed to the floor. The doorway to the emergency stairs had a security camera above it live-streaming to a closed-circuit security monitor at the main desk. The door opened, and he proceeded down the stairs to the main floor.

CHAPTER 23: WHAT HAVE THEY DONE TO OUR KING?

France, 1547

The captain and his men arrived at Nag's Head as the red-orange glow of the sun's evening light was fading behind the tree line. As they approached, the captain spotted a group of men huddled around the river bank drawing up some fishing nets. Some of the men were putting their catch into sacks of leather.

"Draw swords, men, and charge!" commanded Captain Cotter.

The tired horses gathered all the strength they possessed and carried their riders forward. The sound of heavy horses approaching startled the Frenchmen by the river, as they did not believe that they were going to be caught so soon. Most of them had no weapon ready for the powerful English charge. It was a simple matter; the horsemen were upon the French in no time. As the French soldiers who had been pulling the nets from the river stood, an English blade swung towards each of them and decapitated its intended target. Within seconds, the assault was over. Seven headless bodies lay about the bank as the three Frenchmen who had been filling the sacks raised their arms and dropped their weapons if they had them.

"*Nous nous rendons*! We surrender!" the Frenchmen pleaded in unison.

Cotter dismounted along with his men. They gathered their prisoners and retrieved the leather bags. No effort was made to look after the dead.

"Oh, dear God! Captain," called the verger who was inspecting the confiscated sacks, "look over here. In this bag, sir… bones."

Cotter went over and grabbed the bag from his subordinate and looked inside. He laid the bag on the ground and opened each one quickly to inspect its contents. To his horror, there were the remains of a human skeleton contained in the five large leather bags. A few finger bones still had royal rings attached to them. Even the coronation ring that Henry had worn was among the jewelry. An angry and quiet mood descended on the captain and his men.

"These bastards did this to our king," the verger who had first opened the bags said in disgust.

Two of the three French prisoners began sobbing. They knew full well that retribution was sure to be swift and painful. One of them began to urinate through his chainmail uncontrollably.

"Why do you do this?" hissed Cotter, pointing towards the leather bags.

The gaunt knight who had remained calm looked at the captain with dark sunken eyes. "Your king killed our nobility. Your king killed our brothers, cousins, neighbors, fathers. Even our young squires couldn't escape your butchering army."

Captain Cotter surveyed the three men before him. Only the lean, haggard man seemed to be worthy of the title of "knight." He looked at the French gentleman. Most of the man's armor had been taken off, probably for comfort. Cotter could see the scars on the knight's thin legs and hands, including a healed arrow wound just above the left knee. Captain Cotter pointed at the man's knee with his sword.

"I see an archer once found his mark. What is your family name?"

"Yes, my lord," the French knight responded, "it was a clean hit. My name is Reynauld, the arrow pierced my chainmail and went through the muscle. The arrowhead then stopped a half-inch into my saddle. I was able to break it off neatly and pull the shaft out."

"So," Cotter said, pointing his sword at the three men before him, "now answer my first question."

The three Frenchmen stood silently and bowed their heads.

Angrily, one of the captain's men picked up a bludgeon and clubbed the man who had urinated on himself. The frightened Frenchman fell to his knees, crying and holding the side of his head where he had been hit.

"Answer the captain's question," the soldier with the bludgeon yelled at the three Frenchmen, "or someone is going to die this time."

Still the Frenchmen remained silent with their heads bowed.

"All right! Time for some knocking!" the soldier wielding the club cried out as he raised the large weapon to deliver a killing blow.

"Hold!" Cotter bellowed, causing the clubman to stop his swing in midair.

Reynauld mumbled something softly, and the captain stepped closer, leaning in to hear what the man was saying.

"What did you say?" Cotter asked, tilting his head closer to hear better.

Reynauld's eyes burned with hatred as he looked up at Cotter. "We are known as *La Compagnie des Os*. Your king's body was to be captured, and his bones brought back to our elders. A secret ritual was to be performed. Then your king's bones were to be ground into dust. In doing so, our slain brothers would be avenged and our honor restored."

"The Company of Bones?" asked Cotter.

"We are to shadow your king's remains for eternity, and if the opportunity arises, we are to capture what we can and bring them to our masters."

Captain Cotter stepped back, shaking his head as he raised his sword and pointed it at Reynauld. "Is this some devilry?"

"We serve a different master than you," Reynauld said, his eyes narrowed and his voice filled with venom. "Your king's bones will give our master strength. We are the rightful knights of our guild. We are many fold in number, and we have all sworn this oath. This oath will be fulfilled, and then our destiny will be complete."

"Please tell them no more! The English are evil! They will kill us all!" cried the man that had been bludgeoned. He was still on his knees with his hand rubbing his bruised and bleeding head.

"Shut up, you!" yelled the clubman as he made another hit upon the injured man. This time the club struck home, smashing into the Frenchman's temple. The Frenchman collapsed onto the ground, dead.

"Idiot!" yelled Captain Cotter as he pierced his own man who had swung the club with his sword.

The English soldier clutched his bowels as fell over. He was dead by the time he hit the ground.

The remaining two Frenchmen were aghast at the swift justice for their dead comrade. They realized that the English captain could be trusted.

Cotter pointed his sword at the bags as he looked at his prisoners. "We have all of our king's bones?"

Reynauld nodded in agreement.

"Then I will set you free. You are to return to your masters. You will tell them that you have failed and instruct them that they are to give up on their oaths. The king will be safe from your future actions. I grant you your freedom on these terms. If you return, I will slay you all. This is your only warning."

The two Frenchmen bowed to the captain and gathered their belongings. Then they proceeded down the road and disappeared around the bend. It was dark by that time, and the walk was going to be a long one to the English coast. There, a French ship would bring them home.

After about a half an hour, Reynauld had noticed a large branch on the side of the road in the moonlight. His companion hadn't noticed it and continued walking. Reynauld slowed and picked up the large stick and continued to follow his colleague. After a few more steps, he swung his improvised club. The hit was swift and smashed in the back of the man's head, killing him before his body hit the dirt.

Reynauld dragged his dead comrade into the nearby bushes where he reached down and gently closed the dead man's eyes. "I'm sorry, my friend, but where I am going, you cannot talk about today."

He then continued his trek to France with no remorse. He gently patted the three small bones from the king's foot in his pants' pocket: a toe phalanx, metatarsal, and a third bone he didn't recognized. Those were the only ones he had managed to get before the English attack.

CHAPTER 24: RUSH HOUR

England, 2014

Michael got off the bus at the end of the tour when they pulled into a small hotel chain on the outskirts of London. A line of cabs was ready to be hired at the corner. Michael approached the first one in line and got in.

"Please take me to the Landmark Hotel."

The cabbie nodded and started the meter as he pulled away from the curb and into the steady flow of cars going by. Traffic was moderately heavy as it was quitting time for Londoners. The taxi navigated the traffic with ease as the driver knew some of the more intricate streets to dart around the normal congestion spots. A short time later, they pulled up in front of the large hotel.

"Here we are, sir," the cabbie said, turning in his seat towards Michael. "That will be thirty-three euros."

Michael knew the cab ride would be expensive, but he didn't care. He was tired, hungry, and ready to see his family. He handed the driver the money. "Thanks."

The man nodded back as Michael exited the cab. He walked over to the pizza place across from the hotel. It was already getting busy, so Michael went to the bar and ordered a local stout beer. He then grabbed the last table with four black wooden chairs and sat down. A server brought over a menu, and since he was starving and knew Steve and Elizabeth would be there soon, he went ahead and ordered a couple of pizzas for them.

Michael had about fifteen minutes by himself for some reflection on the mysteries of men dressed as priests, the half-naked body he'd found beneath the desk, the untimely death of the woman he'd met the night before, and David's wooden box with a bone in it. None of it made sense to him. All he'd wanted to do was return the box to David's church, yet it seemed like one bad thing had happened after another since he'd arrived in England. The more he thought about it all, the more he couldn't help but wonder if all the events weren't somehow related. Instinctively, his hand ran over his pants' pocket, feeling to be sure that the box was safe.

He rolled his neck, trying to release the tension that gripped it. As he did, the still-healing wound on his neck hurt, and he winced in pain. He placed his elbows on the table and cradled his head in his hands, closing his eyes. He suddenly felt so alone. His mind wandered to Lake Lanier and the summer days on the water surrounded by his loved ones. The idea of being home was so comforting, and he couldn't help but yearn to be there as the burden of friendship and of a promise to a dying comrade weighed heavily on his heart.

Michael took a deep breath as he lifted his head and opened his eyes. He took the pint glass in his hand and lifted it to his lips to take a long drink of the dark beer. No matter how tempting it was to run home, the sense of duty overwhelmed Michael's moral compass. To alter course to any degree meant the loss of honor in his heart, and that would have been far worse to him than the uncertainty he was confronted with.

CHAPTER 25: A MOUSE AND A MOLE

England, 2014

Elizabeth and Steve were just leaving their hotel room when they saw a young man with dark hair and a jacket standing outside the doorway to the room they were supposed to occupy rattling the doorknob. The man scowled at Elizabeth. His face was youthful, albeit angry, and he had a large mole to the right of his nose, just underneath the nostril.

The man's icy stare shocked Elizabeth, and she paused for a half-second as if she had recognized the man and his mole. He, in turn, stared at her and at Steve. It was if he knew, or was supposed to know, their faces. A sudden chill ran up Elizabeth's spine, and her stomach began to knot.

The angry young man shook his head slightly and turned back to the door and knocked. Elizabeth snapped out of it and hurried after Steve. She couldn't help but notice that the stranger continued to glance at them until she and Steve turned the corner to the elevators, increasing the uneasy feeling in her stomach.

Once safely around the corner, Elizabeth gave her cousin a wide-eyed stare of disbelief as they stopped in front of the elevators. She shrugged her shoulders in silence as she waved her right hand towards the location of the stranger with the mole. Steve rolled his eyes as he pushed the down button. In a brief moment, the elevator chimed and the door opened.

Steve and Elizabeth went into the elevator, and she pushed the button for the street level floor. As the shiny brass doors began to close, a man's voice could be heard as he slipped his hand between the closing elevator doors. "Just a minute!"

Elizabeth screamed and squeezed Steve's arm, terrified that the strange man with the mole was wanting to board their elevator. Steve braced himself for danger and was ready to attack the new boarder. Then, to her relief, the doors opened and it wasn't him. Elizabeth tapped Steve's arm again to signal that it was okay. It was another patron of the hotel from a different room wanting to catch a ride down. Steve let out a small exhale to alleviate his nerves.

"Is everything all right, miss?" asked the stranger as he paused before entering the elevator.

"Yes. Yes, I'm fine. Thank you," Elizabeth lied, her freckled cheeks red with embarrassment.

"She thought she saw a mouse," responded Steve as he remembered a funny scene in a movie just like the one they were currently in.

The man looked nervously at the floor of the elevator, still standing outside with his hand holding the door open. "A mouse?"

"Yes, a mouse. Don't you have any fears?" added Elizabeth. "Can we please go down now?"

The man nodded, still searching the floor of the elevator as he timidly climbed aboard. Steve chuckled, and Elizabeth elbowed him as she shot him a sideways glance. The ride down was made in complete silence, and the man hurried off the elevator before Elizabeth and Steve, still looking down to be sure that there were no mice. Steve burst into laughter, and Elizabeth couldn't help but let out a giggle as they, too, exited the elevator and walked towards the hotel door.

CHAPTER 26: BREAKING NEWS

England, 2014

In no time, Elizabeth and Steve were across the street at the pizzeria. As they walked in, Michael gave them a great big smile and stood to greet them with warm hugs. They all sat down at the little table. Two small pizzas that smelled fabulous were already on the table, as well as three plates. The waitress came over and took a drink order as everyone settled into their seats. She hurried off to get their beers.

"So, how are you feeling?" Steve asked, pointing towards the bandage on Michael's neck. "Things healing, okay?"

Michael half-smiled as his hand cupped the side of his neck briefly. "I'm okay. It bled a little this morning, but I'll make it. I got really lucky…. Three times now, actually. But, how are you guys doing?"

"Steve and I just had the weirdest experience," Elizabeth said before Steve could answer. "We couldn't get our reserved room at the hotel, and then when we were leaving our new room to meet you, there was this guy with a big mole on his face trying to get into that room!"

"Yeah, and Elizabeth screamed like a girl at some other guy when he tried to get on the elevator with us," Steve said, giving Elizabeth a wry look.

"I am a girl," she replied, rolling her eyes. "It was scary. That guy with the mole really creeped me out."

Steve and Michael chuckled as the waitress arrived with a round of beers. Once she left, they all grabbed a slice of pizza and began to eat.

"You said earlier that you got lucky three times, Michael," Steve said between bites of pizza. "What did you mean by that? Was there more than one attack?"

Michael finished his bite of pizza before answering. "No, there was only the one attack in Afghanistan. I got really lucky there. My friend David was in the room with me, and he got killed."

"We're really sorry, Michael," Elizabeth said, smiling kindly at him as she reached out and laid her hand on his. "We hope that having your family with you now will help you through all this."

Michael smiled back meekly. "It does help. I was actually feeling pretty alone 'til you guys showed up. I'm glad you're here."

The three sat in silence for a moment as they ate their pizza. Michael took a long, slow drink of his beer as he looked for the words to tell his family about everything else that had happened. Just having them there was enough to encourage him. He took a deep breath and began.

"As my friend David was dying, he asked me to do him a favor. He had taken a box from the church he attended here in England thinking it would bring him luck, and he asked me to return it."

"Must have been a special box. What was in it?" Steve asked as he grabbed another slice of pizza.

"It is some kind of bone. I'm not sure what kind of bone, but I'm pretty sure it's a human bone, maybe a finger," Michael answered. "When I told him I would return it, he told me not to trust anyone. And, I have to tell you, I'm starting to wonder just how much danger I got myself into when I agreed to do this for him."

"Is that what you meant about being lucky?" Steve asked as Michael nodded in affirmation. "What kind of danger do you mean?"

Michael took a bite of pizza and chewed for a moment. "Well, to start with, last night this girl that was trying to hook up with me got shot in the head right as I bent down to pick up her phone."

"She what?" Elizabeth asked, almost choking on her pizza. Steve slapped her on the back, and she coughed repeatedly.

"She got shot," Michael said in a low voice as he offered Elizabeth her beer to help her stop coughing. "The police haven't found out who did it, either."

Elizabeth laid her pizza slice on the plate as she took the glass. She took a long drink of beer and looked back and forth between Michael and Steve in disbelief.

"And it gets stranger," Michael continued as Steve and Elizabeth leaned in to listen. "This morning, I took the box to the cathedral to give it to the head verger there, a guy named Lark. When I got there, I had a long talk with a really skinny guy I thought was Lark while his associate, this really huge guy in a black cassock that didn't talk, stood there like he was blocking the door. The guy I thought was Lark told me the bone was a bad practical joke on David's part and that it was nothing more than a chicken bone."

"A chicken bone?" Steve asked as he took a sip of beer. "Why would your friend send you on a mission to return a chicken bone?"

"I don't think he did." Michael leaned in and lowered his voice. "You see, I went to the bathroom before I left. I decided to stop back by to ask the guy if I could have the box back just to remember David—he had thrown it in the trash after he told me it was a joke. When the guys weren't there, I bent over to get it out of the trashcan—"

Suddenly, the television on the wall of the restaurant flashed a special bulletin, interrupting Michael. Most people in the restaurant were busy eating and talking, but many paused to hear the announcement, including Elizabeth, Steve, and Michael.

"Ladies and gentlemen, we apologize for interrupting our current program. This is an important BBC announcement of national security," the television reporter announced as the video of a man hurrying from Chelmsford Cathedral played on the screen. "This man is believed to be a Lt. Michael Cotter. He is a United States Army soldier and is wanted for questioning in the assault and brutal murder of the cathedral's head verger, Mr. John Lark."

Steve and Elizabeth looked at Michael and then back to the television where a blurry image of Michael's face filled the screen.

"If you see this man, he is to be considered armed and dangerous," the reporter continued. "Report his whereabouts immediately to the authorities."

"Michael, that's you!" whispered Steve.

"Let's get out of here," Elizabeth said quietly as she put some money on the table to pay for dinner.

As the three hurried to the door, a few of the patrons noticed that the picture on the TV screen looked a lot like Michael, and one person was already dialing on their cellphone.

CHAPTER 27: REMEMBER TO SERVE

England, 2014

The three began to run as the pizzeria door shut behind them. They dashed across the street, darting in and out of traffic, and into the hotel. Once inside, they slowed and walked past the front desk to the elevator. There were several police officers in the lobby, along with some medical personnel and firemen. Police radios squawked back and forth, relaying messages that units were being dispatched to the hotel. Michael held his head down as the elevator door opened and the three hurried inside.

"What is going on?" asked Steve as the elevator door shut behind them.

"It's what I was telling you about," Michael said, keeping his head down to avoid any possible cameras that might be in the elevator. "Trust me, guys. Wait until we get into your room."

When the elevator reached their floor, it opened to a horrific scene. Three stretchers with black plastic body bags were being wheeled out of room 316. Police, medical personnel, and even some members of the hotel's management were in attendance behind the crime scene tape. A hotel guest down the hallway snapped a picture with her cellphone, but she was quickly apprehended by a policewoman who made her delete the picture.

Elizabeth gasped in horror as Steven grabbed her by the arm and pulled her away from the obvious murder scene. They marched towards their room down the hall. Michael was close behind, looking down at the floor as not to raise suspicion. Steve hurriedly opened the door, and they all rushed in and locked the door behind them.

"That was supposed to be our room!" Elizabeth said as soon as the door was closed. She stood there shaking her head. "Those people who were killed. That was supposed to be our room! What is going on?"

"Michael, she's right," Steve said, walking across the room and shutting the curtains on the window. "You said you had gotten involved in something dangerous. You've got to tell us what is going on."

Michael walked over and placed his hands on Elizabeth's shoulders. "Hey, it's going to be all right. I won't let anything happen to you."

"Michael, this is just too much. The people in the room we were supposed to be in are dead. The girl you met last night was killed. The news says you killed that man, Lark. What is going on?" Elizabeth demanded as she laid her head on Michael's chest.

Michael hugged Elizabeth as Steve sat down on the end of his bed.

"Let's piece all this together. You said you went back to see Lark again," Steve said calmly. "That's what you were telling us before the news report. What happened?"

Michael nodded his head and helped Elizabeth over to her bed. "Like I said, I went back to get David's box, but no one was there. When I got it out of the trash, a piece of paper fell on the floor. I went to pick up the paper, and that's when I saw this half-naked guy crammed under the desk. I realized that he must have been the real Lark, but he was already dead."

"So who were the two men you talked to?" Elizabeth asked as she sat on the side of the bed that faced the door.

"I'm guessing they're the men that killed Lark," Michael said as he shook his head. He began to pace back and forth between the beds. "I knew they seemed off somehow. The skinny one that looked like a crow was all too eager to dismiss David as some sort of punk. I should have listened to my gut."

"Why did you run off, though?" Elizabeth asked, bewildered. "You could have called the police, and none of this would be happening."

Michael stopped pacing and pressed his hands against his head. "I don't know. I… I just panicked. I don't know what I was thinking. I just knew I had to get out of there."

"It's okay," Steve said, getting up and walking over to Michael. He placed his hand on his brother's shoulder. "It's going to be okay. You've been through a lot lately. First watching your friend die and then having that girl shot in front of you last night. No wonder you panicked."

"Well, what are we going to do?" Elizabeth asked, her face flushed with worry. "I don't think that the cops are going to buy into the idea that he panicked at this point."

"Look, it was a mistake," Steve said, glancing over at her with a stern look on his face. He turned back to Michael. "We all make them. Now, let's figure this out and decide what we need to do to fix it."

Michael shook his head and took a deep breath. He looked at his brother, finding it hard to believe that Steve was the younger of the two at that moment. He nodded and walked over to sit down on Steve's bed facing Elizabeth. Steve came and sat beside him.

"I've been thinking about it a lot," Michael said. "Before he died, David told me that I should trust no one. He used to tell me that there was more to being a verger than I knew, and I always felt like there was some sort of secret he was wanting to tell me but couldn't. The more I think about all that's happened, the more I think that all of this has to do with this box."

Michael pulled the box from his pocket and showed it to the others. "I think someone was trying to kill me last night, not the girl. And I think that the two men at the cathedral were there for the box. I told the imposters that I was meeting you here, so that makes it even more likely that they thought those people down the hall were you guys. And I think it has to do with some secret related to this box."

"But you said they threw this away," Elizabeth said, reaching over and taking the box from Michael's hand. She opened the lid and inspected the bone inside. "Why do you think they want it?"

"The skinny guy—let's call him Crow—he seemed far too eager to dismiss it. And he tried way too hard to make me think David was playing a joke on me. They made up some excuse about another meeting to get me out of the room, and I think they were going to come back to get the box and the bone after I left."

Elizabeth turned the bone over in her hand and held it out to Steve, who took it and inspected it.

"David was devoted to his church and his position as a verger—more than I can explain. He talked about it all the time, and he made it seem like it was more than just a job. It was like a sacred duty to him. He pleaded with me to bring this box and its contents safely back to his church. He used his dying breath to tell me to trust no one, and the last words he ever said were, 'remember to serve.' I really believe that all this has to do with what he told me about this box."

"Yes, I have to say that it seems like it is all connected. Clearly, the imposters want the box," Steve agreed. "The question is: What do we do now?"

"I don't know. I need to think for a minute," Michael said, shaking his head.

Elizabeth got off the bed and walked over to the nightstand and picked up the TV remote. She turned it on, and the three were immediately hit by a blast of volume from a news story. Worried that someone might hear, Elizabeth dialed down the noise.

"Authorities are now adding three more counts to the murderer suspect Michael Cotter," the reporter announced in front of the blurry image of Michael's face from the earlier broadcast. "A man, woman, and young girl were found murdered in their beds in the lavish hotel, the Landmark. Their names are being withheld until the next of kin has been notified. Reports have informed us that the three are from the United States."

Elizabeth switched off the television. Everyone in the room was silent. Suddenly, Steve's cellphone started to ring. The ringtone was the one for their mother and father.

"It's them," Michael said. "Answer it."

Steve lifted the phone to his ear and pressed the button to answer the call. "Hi, Mom and Dad."

"Are you okay?" Mr. Cotter asked from the other end. "We got a call from a news agency asking if we knew the people murdered in your hotel. They used the last name Cotter. What is going on there?"

Michael grabbed the cellphone from Steve and put it on speaker phone.

"Dad, it's me," Michael said quickly. "I have been caught up in something totally out of hand. My friend in the army, David, you remember him? Well, he was killed at our firebase, and he asked me to deliver this special package to a church. Now everybody thinks I am a murderer."

"Son, listen," Mr. Cotter said calmly. "Do not turn yourself in yet. Let me call our law firm and see what we need to do at this point. I think it's best if you find somewhere safe and stay put for now. Don't go out or try to run from this. It will only make things worse."

"Dad, I've got to finish this for David," Michael replied.

"I know you think that, but I really need you to stay safe right now," his father answered. "Now put Steve on the phone so I can talk to him for a minute."

Michael handed the cellphone to his younger brother. Elizabeth, who had heard the conversation, started to cry. Michael got up and walked over to her. He sat down next to her and wrapped his arm around her as she cried. After another minute on the phone, Steve hung up and looked at his brother and cousin.

"I need to get to Canterbury Cathedral," Michael said as Elizabeth dried the last of her tears. "There was a verger there I remember who told me to come see him anytime if I was in the area and needed help."

"He will turn you in, Michael!" responded Elizabeth.

Michael smiled comfortingly at her. "I have to take that chance."

"I think we need to stay put for the rest of the night," Steve said. "Obviously, everyone thinks those people who were murdered were us, and no one knows we're in this room right now. We need to get some sleep before we do anything else. We can get up really early and head out before the hotel staff really starts working in the morning, and it should be safe for us."

"I think that sounds like a good plan," Michael agreed. "Now, let's try to get some sleep. Maybe tomorrow we can find some answers."

CHAPTER 28: A WOLF IN THE ROOM AND ANOTHER AT THE DOOR

England, 2014

It was not quite five o'clock in the morning, and Michael, Steve, and Elizabeth were already up and ready to go. As Elizabeth stuffed their passports and important items in her shoulder bag, Steve produced a square-shaped black backpack from his suitcase.

"I brought you something from Georgia," Steve said as he handed the backpack to Michael. "It's your Wolfie."

"My very first drone!" Michael opened up the bag and removed the box. He opened it and tested the battery on the drone. "Wow. And it's all charged and ready to go. You know I named my drone in Afghanistan Wolf, too?"

Steve chuckled. "I can believe it."

Steve dug in his suitcase once again and pulled out a few more items. He handed his brother a pair of sunglasses and a cap. The hallway had one camera, and it was primarily aimed towards the elevator area. They knew the stairs would be their safest route, but adding any type of disguise they could would hopefully help them avoid detection.

Michael's text message alert sounded. He pulled it out and looked at the screen. It was another message from Tommy. He could tell by the picture of Tommy and Bernard that had popped up on the screen. Elizabeth looked over his shoulder.

"Hey! I've seen that guy before!" Elizabeth said in alarm. "Let me see that!"

Michael handed her the phone and she enlarged the image on the screen of Tommy and Bernard. "I recognize that guy with the mole. Who is he?"

"That's my friend Tommy's roommate. That's a picture from the other night at the pub," Michael explained. "How do you recognize him? I just met him, myself."

"Yesterday, the guy in the hall," Elizabeth said as she shook her head, still looking at the screen. "This is the guy I told you about that we saw trying to get into the room we were supposed to be staying in—the room where those people were murdered!"

Steve came over and took the phone from Elizabeth. He stared at the image on the screen. "I think she's right. But what would he be doing trying to get into that room?"

"This guy gave me the same creeps that Brian fellow on that pontoon boat back on Lake Lanier did. You remember," Elizabeth said, her eyes wide with anxiety. "He stole our submarine."

Michael didn't say anything in response. He didn't understand why Bernard would be in the hotel, much less be trying to get into the room that his family was supposed to be staying in. It didn't make sense to him.

"We better get moving," Steve said with a nod towards the clock. "The sooner we get out of here, the better."

Michael put on the sunglasses and cap and put on the backpack with his drone it in. Elizabeth put on her sunglasses as well and grabbed her bag. The three took a big breath and walked out of their room. As they made their way down the stairs, Michael kept running through everything he and Bernard had said when they were around each other, trying to find a reason for his new friend to have been in the hotel.

CHAPTER 29: RESTART

England, 2014

Bernhard slipped in the side door of the hotel. It was early in the morning, and he was going to try to retrace Vonyou's footsteps from the day before to see what had been missed. As he headed towards the door to the stairway, it opened slightly and he slipped behind a wall protrusion that separated parts of the lobby.

As he watched from his hiding place, a young woman with red hair and sunglasses stuck her head out of the stairwell and looked around cautiously. She slowly opened the door and then stepped out into the lobby. Two men followed behind her. Despite the cap and sunglasses, Bernard instantly knew one of them was Michael. As they hurried towards Bernard to exit the side door, he pressed himself against the wall, hoping they would not look back.

Once they were past him and out the door, he waited several moments and then slipped out of his hiding spot and out the door after them. Standing in the doorway, he could see them at the end of the street near the front of the hotel flagging down a cab.

He got out his cellphone to call his superiors. His heart was racing from the knowledge that he would have to kill Michael and the others. He also figured that he would probably have to eliminate Tommy, his roommate, as well.

"Report!" Crow snapped on the other end of the cellphone as Bernard peered out from behind the doorway to see a cab pull up to the curb in front of Michael and his companions.

"Vonyou has failed us again. Target has two people accompanying him. They are getting into a cab. I am in a shadow pursuit. Do I have new instructions?" Bernard said quietly as he watched the three talking to the cab driver.

"Close the file on Vonyou," Crow ordered. "We will give you his coordinates. Once that file is closed, we will then send you in to finish what Vonyou could not."

"And what of the target? They are speeding away in cab."

"We have an idea where they are headed." The call ended on the other end.

Bernard slid the phone into his pocket and smiled as he turned down the street towards the subway station. He had to prepare so that he would not fail as Vonyou had.

CHAPTER 30: EVIL HAS A SHADOW

England, 2014

Crow hung up the call with Mole and put away his cellphone in his cassock pocket. He was still wearing the verger outfit that he had stolen from the dead man that he had stuffed underneath the desk the day before. He lifted a cup of coffee and took a slow sip as he looked out the window of the small restaurant that he and his partner Muzzy had been waiting at for news.

"How can you be so certain that Michael still has the bone?" asked Muzzy as he, too, sipped his coffee. "Where do you think he is headed?"

"He is looking for answers to his dead friend's last request. He still has the bone, and it looks as if he will lead us to the place that we might find some, if not all, of the bones we are seeking," Crow said as a sinister smile pulled at the edges of his thin lips. "There is one natural location that has always been at the front of our searches, but its secrets have always alluded us. Canterbury!"

Muzzy nodded as a waitress brought over their breakfast plates and dropped them off at the table. She smiled at the two men she thought were clergymen, but they both scowled at her in return and she hurried off.

"Now, send Mole the coordinates he needs," Crow said as he picked up a piece of toast and snapped it in half. "It's about time to go to church."

CHAPTER 31: LET'S GO TO CHURCH

England, 2014

A cab ride, a train ride, and finally another cab ride later, Michael, Steven, and Elizabeth arrived at Canterbury Cathedral. During the trip there, Michael had retold the others the story about how he had gotten lost on the cathedral's grounds and how he had been helped by a verger there. They walked towards the grand cathedral, carefully looking around to be sure that no one recognized Michael.

"Hey, I need to use the restroom," Steve said quietly as they stopped near the front of the cathedral.

"Me, too!" Michael and Elizabeth replied in unison.

The three smiled and found the building adjacent to the cathedral that housed the restrooms, offices for the grounds keeping crew, and the ticket booths during the tourist season.

Michael and Steve entered the men's room. They thought that they were the only ones in there, but an elderly gentleman who was finishing mopping the floor emerged from a stall at the end of the restroom as they were finishing using the bathroom. Michael lifted his sunglasses in alarm and turned around to see who was behind them.

"Careful when you walk," the old man cautioned. "The floors are wet."

As he spoke, the old man's eyes met Michael's and then his memory kicked in like the snap of a finger.

"I know who you are. I remember you," the elderly custodian said.

Steve was already washing his hands and looked at Michael in the washroom's mirror. Michael pulled his sunglasses back over his eyes and ducked his head as he hurried over to wash his hands, as well. The two brothers were at a crossroads with the old man. They knew he was probably referring to the fake news stories of Michael being a murderer.

Michael finished washing his hands and turned toward the custodian. "I can explain...."

The older man put down his mop and walked up to Michael and Steve. He held out his hand to Michael as if to offer a handshake.

"You are that young fellow I helped out inside the cathedral many years ago," the grey-haired man said with a smile. "You are a verger from Georgia, right?"

"Yes, sir," Michael replied, nodding his head as he took the custodian's hand and shook it. "But, how do you remember me from so long ago?"

"Michael. Ah, yes, I remember. Your name is Michael." The man chuckled as he extended his hand to Steve who also shook it. He then turned and headed towards the door. "Come outside where I can see you better."

Michael and Steve looked at each other in amazement and then followed the man outside. Elizabeth had already left the ladies' restroom and proceeded to join Michael and Steve.

"Yes, that's right" Michael said. "This is my brother, Steve, and here comes my cousin, Elizabeth."

The group walked slowly to a grand tree in one of the courtyards of the cathedral. A medium-sized trash bin stood underneath the tree. The custodian opened the trashcan and scooped up a good amount of birdseed that he then sprinkled in the area. Birds of all types flocked to the newly discovered food. Even a few black-winged crows joined in the feast.

"Hello to Michael's family. My name is Phillips," the elderly man said as he sat down beneath the tree. "I am the custodian, grave digger, gardener, wild bird caretaker, and even a porter—what you Americans call a verger—if needed. Welcome to you all."

Michael, Steve, and Elizabeth looked back and forth at each other and then sat down on the grass near Phillips.

"I remember Michael here a long time ago. I thought he was part of a group from Texas. The next thing I knew," Phillips said with a chuckle, "he was a verger and had a group of about twenty Episcopalians on pilgrimage wanting to attend an afternoon mass."

The group laughed because they had already heard the story so many times before.

"So, Michael," Phillips said in a serious tone, "what brings you to see me?"

CHAPTER 32: TERMINATING A FILE

England, 2014

Vonyou didn't like his current location at all. He had been instructed to go to a church near Trafalgar's Square, but something didn't feel right. He double-checked his cellphone for any new texts. There was a new text saying to proceed behind the church.

Vonyou walked briskly to the rear of the church where a service door entrance with a reinforced concrete awning offered a bit of shelter from the early afternoon sun. The church appeared to be closed, and there were no cars in the alleyway.

Vonyou reached into his coat pocket and pulled out a cigarette. He knew the smoke smelled very offensive to those not used to the French brand. He lit the cigarette anyway, inhaled, and blew out the smoke.

"You know that cigarettes will kill you, right?" asked a mysterious voice.

Vonyou was startled. He recognized that voice and frantically looked around for the owner. His free hand reached into a pocket for his pistol.

"Aww, too bad," said the mysterious voice.

In an instant, two black-sleeved arms reached down like a black spider grabbing its prey from the concrete overhang of the doorway and slit Vonyou's throat with an elongated scalpel. The swift action made no sound. The victim was cut in such a way that he could neither breathe nor speak.

Vonyou dropped both his cigarette and pistol as his hands instinctively reached up to hold his wound. His brain began to shut down as the blood gushed from the open veins that carried the vital fluid to the head. He collapsed very quickly.

Bernhard climbed down from his hiding spot and checked Vonyou's pulse to assure he was dead. He then rolled two large gray garbage bins over to conceal the body.

Bernard stepped on the dropped cigarette to put it out, and he picked up Vonyou's pistol. Looking up and down the alley to make sure nobody had witnessed his craftsmanship, Bernhard proceeded back up the street and headed towards the square. He texted as he walked that the file had been terminated and asked what his new orders were.

CHAPTER 33: A VISIT TO THE UNDERCROFT

England, 2014

The birds enjoying the free meal that the custodian had thrown about were uneasy about one of the crows. The robins and pigeons flapped their wings in protest at the large bird eating what was usually their meal for the day. The large crow paid them no heed, for it had another mission: to observe the humans as they talked.

"Well, sir," Michael began, looking at Phillips hesitantly, "I seem to be on a mission to deliver an item entrusted to me by a fellow verger. He was a friend of mine and died serving in the British army in Afghanistan. He asked me to take it to the cathedral in Essex to return it to a man named Lark. My friend said Lark would know what to do. But Lark was murdered, and I think someone is trying to kill me and my family to get the item I am supposed to return."

"Here, let me see it," said Phillips quietly.

Michael carefully pulled out the wooden box from his pants' pocket and handed it to the elderly man.

"Oh, my," Phillips said as he opened the box and looked inside. He quickly shut the lid and covered the box with his other hand as he looked up at Michael. "You shouldn't be in possession of this royal artifact. It belongs in a special place—a special place that only a few know about. You three need to come with me."

"Are we in trouble?" asked Elizabeth.

"No, no, not in the least," Phillips said as he stood up and placed the box in his pocket. "You three are heroes. Now come along. We have work to do."

Michael, Steve, and Elizabeth stood and followed Phillips as he walked to the rear area of the cathedral grounds. The group walked about a hundred yards into a hilly pasture where no other people were. The ground there was hard with a large ditch that lay hidden from the surface view. The group proceeded down into the ditch, safely out of sight from any area on the cathedral grounds. Phillips was a little winded and turned to the others.

"I want each of you to swear to me an oath that will be kept by you for the rest of your lives," he said, his face serious and his tone stern.

Michael looked at Steve and Elizabeth. They all nodded to each other in agreement and then turned to Phillips. Michael said, "We will."

Phillips nodded in return. "Now, raise your right hand and extend your left hand in the middle and lock hands together."

The three awkwardly followed Phillips' instructions and placed their hands accordingly.

"*Me serve et fidelis*," Phillips said in Latin.

The group swore the oath.

"May you always remember it," Phillips said and then patted each one on the cheek, similar to the way knights and monks used to do to their new charges when they gave them a hard slap to shock the brain into remembering the oath.

The group then made the sign of the cross.

With that, Phillips turned his attention to the grassy mound in front of him. "This was originally a Roman wall surrounding their temple. We were able to dig under it."

He then pushed aside some wheat grass to expose a large door in the side of the ditch. Perfectly camouflaged from the surface and from the air, it was very old. Phillips had a large key strapped to his belt and used it to unlock the very heavy metal and wood door. Surprisingly, it opened easily, and the group followed Phillips inside. The large crow observed the humans going into the tunnel; then it flew back to the cathedral's bell tower and perched.

The tunnel that lay behind the door was very dark inside once the door was shut behind them. It had a lingering smell of stale air and mold. Slowly, the group went deeper into the tunnel as they followed Phillips. They eventually reached a lighted hallway that headed back towards the cathedral.

"What is this tunnel?" asked Steve.

"It is a sally port, or what we call a priest's hole. An escape tunnel should the cathedral be attacked. It was dug during the English Civil War in the 1600s to protect the clergy from rampaging iconoclasts. This one leads to the crypts," Phillips responded.

"An undercroft?" Michael asked.

"I imagine you Americans think of it as a basement or a dungeon," Phillips said, glancing over his shoulder with a slight smile. "However, we use crypts for storage, for special deceased members of our church, for an undercroft, and even for offices. Mine is just down this path. That's where we are going to find out this artifact's true location."

The group walked along the cut-stone floors. The entire crypt section with its stone walls was an immense, dimly lit maze with ornate wooden gates and doors that guarded the entrances to each room, vault, or hallway.

"Do all cathedrals have one of these?" asked Elizabeth.

"No, not all of them," Phillips responded. "Ely Cathedral is built on a swampy terrain. The water table was too high to dig an undercroft or crypt."

Phillips turned a corner in the hallway and proceeded a few yards further into a darker part. Illuminated only by the lamps in the main hall, one could barely make out a door. It was wooden with heavy iron fittings and hinges. Phillips produced his key again and turned the tumbler counterclockwise. A heavy deadbolt moved inside the door, and then Phillips turned the key another complete rotation to unlock another tumbler with the lock. That time a smaller knock could be heard as the deadbolt moved into a recessed space within the lock. That allowed full access into the room. Anything less than the timed turns on the lock would have caused the tumblers to lock completely. It was a well-kept secret to the master verger who occupied the chamber.

The group entered, and Phillips produced a light for everyone to see.

The room was as big as an average living room. It had a curved ceiling to support the cathedral's weight above. The walls were stone blocks as well, but they were adorned with several maps of the United States, France, Italy, and the United Kingdom. The maps were marked with different-shaped stars that represented cities, towns, and villages. London, New York, Washington, D.C., Paris, Rome, and smaller town were all marked with stars on the maps. Made from a tanned leather, these stars had been used over the centuries in that very room to mark key items that were sacred and important to Phillips' order.

"What is this place?" asked Elizabeth.

"My dear," Phillips said as he turned to face the group, "this is our map room that keeps track of our king."

"But England has a queen," Steve said, not following the older man's meaning.

"You're quite right, Steve," Phillips said as he sat down in a large wooden chair at the side of the room. "I am referring to the first king of our faith, His Most Royal Highness, Henry VIII."

CHAPTER 34: WHAT'S IN THE BOX?

England, 2014

Michael, Steve, and Elizabeth stood in silence. The full weight of what Phillips had just told them slowly worked its way into their understanding. No one spoke for what seemed like eternity.

"This bone that has been in your possession is one of the most sacred bones of our beloved king," Phillips said as he pulled the box from his pocket and opened it. "It is the phalanges of the ring finger of his right hand. That same finger has been blessed by the Pope and our Church of England."

Michael looked at Steve and Elizabeth who seemed dazed by what was happening. He shook his head, unsure that he had heard correctly himself.

"You three Americans are known as Episcopalians, yet we are all part of the Anglican church," Phillips said as he stood up and placed the box back in his pocket. He slowly walked over to the wall and pointed to a location on the map of the United Kingdom. "The large star you see on the map is where the cathedral of Chelmsford lies. That is where this bone was currently stationed. Your David had been instructed to transfer the bone to Essex."

Michael and the others followed Phillips finger as it moved across the map.

"We rotate the bones every eight years to hide their location," Phillips explained. "It also gives other approved Anglican—and certain Episcopal churches—a chance to share in the wonderful responsibility of protecting their benefactor."

"So the bone is a holy relic?" asked Michael.

"Yes and no," the old verger said, turning to face Michael. "Yes, because Henry was the spiritual leader of our church. Churches throughout the

Middle Ages and up until now used these and many other saints' relics for religious, political, and even military purposes. From teeth, hair, blood, bone, to even dust, all were displayed to bring the faithful closer to God."

Michael nodded. Steve and Elizabeth wandered around the room examining the items on the walls as Phillips continued.

"You must admit, it is good business when pilgrims from all over the world come to see and pay homage to some long-gone saint. Many a church's coffers have been filled in this manner. Sadly, I know many of these saints' relics in England and France that are merely kept in a spare room or, worse, in a forgotten part of the basement or undercroft of some bypassed church."

"So, what did you mean when you said, 'Yes and no'?" Michael asked. "I understand the yes, but what about the no?"

"No, because his bones have become a spiritual target because of their importance in a war against a darker enemy," answered Phillips.

"Who is the older gentleman in this frame over here?" Elizabeth asked from across the room, interrupting Michael and Phillips' conversation.

Phillips walked over to the portrait. "Ah, that's J.P. Morgan from New York. He was a great Episcopalian and possibly the greatest benefactor of our cause. His father was a fine rector for the church in the United States. J.P. admired his father's faith, and when he acquired his millions through the 1920s in oil, J.P. Morgan shared his wealth with the holy church."

Michael and Steve walked over to look at the portrait as well.

"J.P. was a significant member of the church, serving as a lay person and vestry, and it was even rumored that he was a special member of the Verger's Guild. He paid for the construction of a few churches in Europe, such as the one in Rome, St. Paul's Within the Walls," Phillips continued. "The main mural in the nave has St. Paul and St. Augusta in a holy portrait talking to the masses. As a flaunt to the power of the Verger's Guild, the faces of the two saints were of actual members of the guild, not from actual biblical portraits."

As Phillips spoke, Michael continued to ponder the strange turn of events and the unforeseen direction his mission from David had taken. He thought back to David's words telling him to serve, and he could not help but wonder if David had purposefully set him on the next part of his journey as a verger and servant to his church.

"Morgan also paid for the construction of St. James in Florence as well. He insisted that these churches and others like them were to have a secret undercroft for the hiding of Henry's bones, should that church be included in the circle of special caches," Phillips continued. "Why, he even instructed the architects to create special gargoyles crafted in stone! The hideous three-headed creatures were mounted in the middle of a pillar and were believed to be cursed to ward off different evils. They were placed so as to be level with any druid trying to enter the undercroft's stairway, making the undercrofts the perfect refuge for bone storage. Currently, the undercrofts are now refuges for immigrants fleeing Syria."

"Why keep the bones separate and hidden?" asked Michael, bringing the conversation back to the thoughts that were running through his mind.

"The victorious battle His Majesty fought against the French in 1513 resulted in an ugly massacre where his forces stripped and butchered the French army of their wealth and their dignity, even after they had surrendered," the elderly verger explained. "The king's order to 'grind their bones' was a rallying cry that got carried away. The French survivors pledged a dark pact to an ancient, godless evil in the woods of France for revenge. To feed this evil throughout the ages, these dark forces constantly seek out the king's bones. It is believed they even employ the services of the genus *Corvus*."

"*Corvus*?" asked Michael.

"Crows and ravens," Phillips responded as he walked across the room towards the chair he had sat down in earlier. "Some in France mockingly refer to ravens as the souls of wicked priests, while crows are the souls of wicked nuns. Whatever they are, the *Corvus* genus is a highly advanced species that rivals the dolphin and the chimpanzee in problem solving."

Michael looked at Steve and Elizabeth. He had a hard time believing that crows and ravens could be employed for evil service, but he had also not been prepared for the fact that the box he had been sent to deliver actually contained the finger bone of King Henry VIII. Steve and Elizabeth looked just as confused as he was, but he shrugged and smiled to encourage them that it could be possible.

"At one time," Phillips said as he stopped in the center of the room and turned to the others, "these dark knights stole the king's whole body, but some of Henry's vergers and guards rescued the bones that remained. The dark knights called themselves the Company of Bones at that time, an evil that still plagues us. They have only a few of his bones in their possession, which are considered lost to us forever. They even have some sacrificial stone mill waiting to grind King Henry's bones into dust. What they plan to do to his dust is only known to them."

"So, your job is to keep the bones separate and hidden so that these dark forces don't complete their quest?" asked Steve.

Phillips nodded in silence and motioned for the group to join him.

As the group collected themselves in the center of the map room, a strange tapping could be heard from a small door recessed into the stone wall.

"Quiet, Caesar. Quiet," Phillips said, glancing towards the door. "We have special guests with us today."

Michael, Steve, and Elizabeth were puzzled by the unusual communication from their host to the noise emanating from the small wooden door. It had specially drilled holes ornately arranged to form several small groups of circles in threes. The average observer would suspect a three-leaf clover design. To the Christian faithful, it was known as a trefoil, which symbolized the Holy Trinity. The group then noticed a large black beak poke through one of the air holes. Several caws sounded as the occupant wanted to be released.

"Caesar?" asked Michael.

"Ah, yes," Phillips said with a smile, "meet my extraordinary friend."

CHAPTER 35: PROTECT, SAVE, SERVE

England, 2014

Phillips walked over to the wall and then pulled up the heavy metal latch that opened the wooden door. He then offered his arm like a gentleman offering his arm to escort a lady to the dance floor.

Caesar, a very large raven, walked to the edge of his cage and hopped onto Phillips' arm. He waved his wings as if to stretch and greet his guests.

"Where did you get this raven?" Elizabeth asked, stepping closer to get a better look at the large, black bird. "Is he one of the famous ravens from the Tower of London?"

"Indeed, young lady," Phillips said, sitting down in the chair against the wall. "Caesar here is rumored to be as old as 500 years, maybe more."

"Impossible," protested Steve, shaking his head adamantly. "Not a raven. A tree maybe, but not an old bird."

"This isn't any old bird, young sir," Phillips said, extending his arm across a table that was near the chair against the wall. "Caesar is one of a kind—unique—and blessed by some certain life force that has kept him around for a long time."

With that, Caesar jumped off of Phillips' arm and onto the table. The large bird walked over to a plate that held some water to take a drink. Next, the bird stepped into the water to wet his feet. He cawed three times and then proceeded to a saucer that had some dried black pen ink. Dipping his leathery feet into the dried ink, he rotated from one claw to the other, like a winemaker pressing grapes with his feet in a barrel. Quickly, the dried ink became liquid and adhered to Caesar's feet. Phillips, realizing what his feathered friend was doing, produced a large sheet of parchment from a drawer under the front of the table and laid it on the tabletop. Soon the raven began to walk upon the paper.

Michael, Steve, and Elizabeth walked over to watch the bird.

"What's he doing?" Elizabeth asked, tilting her head to the side as she watched.

"Wait and see," responded Phillips with a chuckle. "This will surprise you all."

The black ink scratches made by Caesar's feet made marks on the paper. It truly looked as if a two-year-old had gotten hold of his granddaddy's ink pen and started scribbling.

"Now, behold," whispered Phillips, leaning in to watch as Michael and the others did the same.

A very special dance of the markings began to take form on the paper. The scratches moved magically across the parchment and took shape. Soon the marks began to form into letters. Letters became words, and words then formed a sentence: *I AM... THE KING'S BIRD... PROTECT... SAVE... SERVE.*

"I am the king's bird. Protect, save, serve?" asked Michael as he straightened and looked back and forth between the elderly verger and raven before him.

Caesar instantly let out four loud caws meaning "yes" or "good." He then wrote one more set of scratches. It transformed into *PLEASE*.

At that moment, everyone laughed, easing the unusual and bizarre moment.

CHAPTER 36: AN UNHOLY CHARGE

France, 1579

There were many types of druid orders. Some were kind and benevolent, while others had a darker, more sinister aspect to their religion. The druid order that Reynauld was about to address, furious over being displaced by the new Christian faith sweeping France and other parts of Europe, was one of the darker sects. Seeking refuge in the wilds of forgotten forests and swamps, they held fast to the old ways.

The English king, Henry VIII, had been the druids' scourge. His armies had decimated their lands and forced them to go on the defensive. Their congregation of followers were either dying off from age or converting over to this new faith, so the order had devised a plan. By using the French defeat, Cassandra was to have sealed a bargain with King Henry to stop the persecution of their druid order and return their lands back to their control. When this had failed, they had been forced to develop a new plan.

In a small circular clearing deep within a dark French forest, Reynauld and Cassandra arrived to give their report to the druid council. The enormous trees that surrounded the glade on all sides seemed to interlace their branches as soon as the two entered the clearing, imprisoning Reynauld and Cassandra as they walked to the center of the small open space. Reynauld stopped before a large stump and turned in a circle to watch their imprisonment, and Cassandra set down a wooden cage that she had brought with her to do the same.

Two ancient sessile oaks that were covered with ferns and moss stood across from each other on either side of the clearing. Reynauld and Cassandra watched as the oaks' large branches reached out, growing and stretching as they encircled one portion of the clearing and intertwined to form a strange semicircular table with seats. As the last branches laced together, a shadowy council of five druid elders emerged from the trees surrounding the table. Wrapped in Spanish moss like whispers of smoke, the council seemed to float out of the trees themselves. As they approached the semicircular table, the greenish-blue wraiths took on a more rigid form. The ancient beings carefully slid into the seats formed from the ancient oaks' branches and eyed their visitors suspiciously.

"Why have you returned?" hissed the mysterious druid who sat at the center seat of the table. "Where are Henry's bones you promised us?"

"The king's men discovered us by the river," Reynauld answered sheepishly. "They killed every one of my men. I alone survived."

"He speaks the truth," confirmed Cassandra, nodding her head.

"Perhaps, you should join them?" asked the center druid who seemed to be the leader of the council.

"No, wait! Please!" Reynauld protested, his gaunt face growing white with fear. He pulled several small items from his pants' pocket and held out his hand towards the council. "I have brought you these three bones from his body!"

"Retrieve them!" ordered the druid leader.

Immediately, several druids in hooded robes emerged from the surrounding trees and approached the trembling French knight. Like simple street beggars, they grabbed the rare treasure of bones from his hand. They carried them over and dropped them onto the stump before the semicircular table where the druid council sat.

Another druid stepped out of the trees, carrying a large knife fashioned from the antler of a great stag. He was their high priest, and he walked over to the stump and drug the knife across its round top. The screeching of the blade echoed through the still air. The knife and stump served as a sacrificial altar and had been washed many times in the blood of the druids' multiple offerings to their spirits. Cassandra was in their order, and she was one of the most devout to their way of life. She silently moved away from the altar into the background to observe her master's judgement, leaving Reynauld to be the first to face his wrath should it prevail.

The knife, held in the hand of the high priest, touched the bones displayed on the stump. The dark blade gave off a faint, sickly glow, confirming the bones were indeed part of Henry's body. The high priest bowed to the council in approval of the sacrifice as he slid the knife into his robe.

"Excellent! Begin with the ceremony at once!" demanded the leader of the druid council.

Four druids came forth from the trees behind Reynauld and Cassandra with an ancient stone mill. Cassandra moved back to her place beside Reynauld as the heavy mill was set up. After the mill was prepared, three of the four druids retreated into the trees again.

The three-foot granite wheel rotated in a vertical position on a dark brown, rusted iron frame with a crank handle at one side. The remaining druid turned the crank counterclockwise. This made the wheel hum with an evil, resonating energy, an energy that cracked and moaned as the wheel was turned in reverse as if it was turning back the hands of time. The aura around the ceremony was unnerving to the knight.

The high priest raised a single bone high for all to see. Then the bone was carried over and placed against the moving grist mill. The mill's hum intensified as the bone was being ground into dust. It was as if the stone in the mill was alive and enjoying some tasty morsel. A wooden pail was below to catch all of the dust that fell. The druid high priest muttered obscure and unintelligible words and phrases as the grinding continued. The French knight began to tremble in fear of the evil magic taking place.

As soon as the first bone of Henry's was destroyed, a second one was brought forth to the grinding stone. The procedure continued until the third bone was ground up as well. When all of the bones were destroyed, the druid who had been turning the crank gathered the bucket and handed it to the high priest. The other druids who had brought forth the millstone came forth from the trees again with several bottles which they placed on the stump altar before retreating into the trees again. The high priest made a terrible concoction in the pail containing the bone dust by adding in a mixture of a foul wine, water, and ingredients known only to the druids.

The high priest looked at Cassandra and motioned for her to come forth. She hurried over and produced a raven from the wooden cage that she had brought with her. She handed the large black bird to the high priest. The priest held the bird's beak open while two other druids came forward. One druid produced a funnel and placed it in the bird's mouth. The other poured the mixture from the pail into the funnel, forcing the raven to swallow the liquid. The bird coughed and choked on the nasty fluid.

Another druid came forward from the trees with a saucer filled with dark liquid and a large piece of parchment. He placed them on the altar. The raven was then made to stand in the saucer filled with black ink. From there, the bird was then placed on the piece of paper. The druids all waited anxiously to see if the spell had taken hold.

Within a minute, the bird had walked a few steps, leaving simple bird footprints on the paper. Everyone watched the raven's travels on the parchment. The scratches began to move, and cryptic and indecipherable words began to take shape faintly from them. As quickly as they had begun to form, however, the magically enhanced markings soon reformed back into the footprints of the raven. It was a disappointment for the druids.

"Blah!" cried the leader of the druid council as his glare turned icy. "Your bird is worthless, Cassandra!"

"You need more bones in the potion to make it work! Bones that have more marrow in them," countered Cassandra as she cowered before the sinister being before her.

"What we need is the king's ring finger!" the high priest offered, boldly speaking up for his faithful follower before ducking his head in fear of what such insolence might bring.

"I agree!" said Cassandra, nodding her head vehemently. "We need the ring finger."

The leader of the druid council carefully pondered the idea. He turned to his fellow council members and spoke in a strange language known only to the elders of the druid order. After several minutes of discussion, all five members of the council nodded their hooded heads in agreement. The leader of the council looked from Cassandra to Reynauld, whose heart froze in his chest as the ancient being's eyes pierced into his soul.

"My brethren," hissed the druid council leader, "let us charge this French knight, Sir Reynauld Entienne, the last surviving member of *La Compagnie des Os*, with the solemn task of forming a new guild. This guild, with its followers for centuries to come, will pursue and bring to us the king's bones, piece by piece."

Reynauld looked on solemnly as every member of the council nodded in agreement.

"The ring finger will be your ultimate goal," the council leader continued. "The dust will continue to be gathered and transmuted. Our great spell to change the world to follow our great spirits will one day be complete. Reynauld Entienne, you and all your descendants and followers will honor and fulfill the oath you are about to take to this cause. With your soul as an eternal hostage for ransom, do you so swear?"

Reynauld, trapped into making an oath he did not understand nor want to follow, felt the pressure of an imaginary rough-hewn blade slowly scratching across his neck as if to remind him what might happen if he refused.

Reynauld bowed his head and placed his hand on his heart. "I swear this oath."

The druid elders approved this action with a nod of their heads.

"Cassandra," the druid leader hissed, turning to the elderly witch before him, "we charge you to follow this oath through. Do not fail us. No matter how long it will extend your druid life, do not fail us."

Cassandra acknowledged her charge with a nod of her head and changed form back into an old crow. She then flew off through the opening in the trees above. Reynauld quickly gathered his wits as a path in the same general direction as the bird had flown opened up in the trees. He bowed to his masters and left to pursue the fulfillment of his oath.

In the years to follow, Reynauld Entienne assembled the most unsavory types throughout France to join his guild, which became known as the *Os Legentis*, or Bone Gatherers. His band of men and women, some druid and others non-believers who served for pay, scoured the French countryside, England, and abroad to find Henry's bones. Churches, cathedrals, and monasteries were secretly infiltrated and searched. Through grottoes, undercrofts, basements, and cemeteries, the search for Henry's bones continued.

At first, the Bone Gatherers looked for the entire skeleton of Henry. This went on for several decades, but it proved more elusive than originally planned. Then, one day, upon the death of a clergyman connected to Henry's reign, one of Reynauld's followers found out that another secret guild had been formed to protect their dead king by separating his bones and scattering them throughout the Christian world.

By that time, Reynauld had died, and it was Reynauld's son who was then cursed with the unnatural and evil oath. At one point, he had tried to stop the search, only to have Cassandra infiltrate his mind and convince him otherwise. Generation after generation took the oath, some voluntarily and others not. Even when Reynauld's descendants had vanished, Cassandra kept the pace by recruiting new followers. The curse from her druid brethren had doomed not only Reynauld, but her as well. Sadly, her lifespan would continue as if time were standing still until all the bones were found.

CHAPTER 37: CASSANDRA'S RING

England, 2014

Bernard's cellphone began to ring, and he quickly answered.

"Yes," he said as Crow gave him his next orders from the other end of the line. "Yes, I understand. Canterbury Cathedral immediately. I am on my way."

Bernard's face was filled with resolution and determination that this was the final moment, the moment that his guild had long awaited. He slid his phone into his pocket and hailed a taxi to take him to the nearest car rental place.

As the cab sped down the streets of London, he solemnly gazed upon a special ring he proudly wore. It was his guild ring that had been given to him secretly by an older lady named Cassandra. She was a rather distinctive-looking old woman, as if she had experienced the world over and over again. She had given the gold ring to him and told him he was then one of many.

Bernard knew he had found his place. The ring was special. By it, he was being recognized by a society that appreciated efficiency, a society that rewarded him handsomely for his work. Such rewards were far more satisfying than the dull computer software job he had with Tommy.

"Yes, I earned this," he said softly as he rotated the ring around his finger.

The ancient words engraved along the top were flanked by a crow on one side and a raven on the other. They read: *"Memento quod ossium."*

"Remember the bones," he whispered as the cab pulled into the car rental place.

CHAPTER 38: THE RAVEN SAYS YES

England, 2014

Michael, Steve, and Elizabeth looked at each other and then back to the elderly man and raven before them. The laughter they had just shared had settled their nerves. Michael felt more certain than ever that David had sent him on the mission to return the bone to discover the very things that they had just discovered. Still, there were questions that remained.

"You said that these maps help you keep track of the king, but how do they do that?" Michael asked as he gestured towards the various maps that adorned the stone walls.

"The maps in this room are a vital part of our defense," Phillips said, rising from his chair and walking over to one of the maps. "Each star indicates the location of one of the bones of our great king. We make pilgrimages to these locations, and we are constantly looking for new locations to house the bones."

"How do you do that?" Michael asked as he joined Phillips in front of the map.

"When a possible new location has been discovered, we recruit and insert our people into that parish," Phillips replied. "It takes about a year to complete the process. The basement, undercroft, or even a well-protected sacristy will be thoroughly searched and observed by our inserted verger. If the church has signage on doors or hallways giving directions, any reference to the secret location will be taken down."

Steve and Elizabeth walked over to join them as they looked at the maps.

"If his bones are spread all over the place," Elizabeth asked, "who's buried in that crypt with Charles I?"

"I am very impressed, young lady, that you knew that. Not very many people do," Phillips said with a chuckle as he turned and looked at Elizabeth. "It is a very secret ruse, my dear, that fooled our enemies for years. The body buried there is actually one of Henry's men who died defending his king. Even now, that verger's bones are still protecting Henry."

"So, people truly are still trying to steal the bones?" Michael asked.

"Yes, they most certainly are," Phillips said with a nod. He walked back to his chair and sat down. "Thieves actually stole the skull of King Charles thinking it was that of Henry, even though it was later found. They are called the Bone Gatherers now, and I believe that is the group that you have found yourself entangled with."

Michael nodded his head as he walked over to where Phillips sat and took off his backpack. He knew for certain that all his suspicions were true about the mission he was on for David being the reason for the strange events of the past three days. He exhaled as the true meaning of his journey sank in, and he knew that his duty was no longer just to his friend, but to his church.

"This information that you've given us—this room, even—is such an important secret to our church. Why are you telling us? How do you know you can trust us?" Steve asked the elderly verger as he and Elizabeth came to stand beside Michael.

"I didn't completely know if I could trust you at first," Phillips admitted with a slight shake of his head. "But once we were here, I knew I could trust you."

"How?" Michael asked, just as curious as his brother to know the answer.

"It is because of Caesar," Phillips said with a smile as the black bird let out a loud caw. "He senses both good and evil. He has lived throughout the years, and the spell that keeps him alive also guides his judgement. Our enemies have many times tried to infiltrate our guild. Caesar has the ability to see through people and judge quickly the good from the bad. There have been several men claiming to be vergers who weren't. To this day, Caesar has caught every one of them."

The raven walked across the table and flapped its large wings as it let out four loud caws. Phillips reached out his hand and stroked the bird's head.

"When Caesar wrote to tell you to protect and serve, he was acknowledging your allegiance to good rather than evil," Phillips said and gave the group a weak smile. "I am dying, but Caesar will live on. The oath I made you three swear is for this very purpose. Protect our king, protect these relics, and serve."

Caesar flapped his wings again as if to strike home the point made by Phillips.

"We will do our best to protect and serve," Elizabeth said as she put her arms around her cousins who were on either side of her.

As if on cue, Michael and Steve took their hands and messed up Elizabeth's red hair.

"We are in this together," Michael said with a smile.

CHAPTER 39: THE HUNTERS BEGIN TO CLOSE IN

England, 2014

Crow and his accomplice arrived by car at Canterbury's parking lot. The dead verger's auto had served its purpose of getting them there as quickly as possible.

"My legs are killing me," grumbled Muzzy as he climbed out of the tiny car and rubbed legs.

Crow climbed out and straightened his black verger's cassock. He then secretly stored his pistol in an inside pocket. The large crow on the bell tower cawed several times as if giving out instructions to the men below.

"Come on and quit your bitching," Crow snapped. "We have work to do."

The two men dressed as clergy walked the pebbled path to the cathedral's office. Both men looked up to see the tremendous size of the church.

The immense Canterbury Cathedral, with its glorious medieval architecture dating back centuries, stood before them. Using only tools of the period—hammers, chisels, and rudimentary gangways and cranes—the architects had built a wondrous glory to God. The cathedral was built horizontally in the shape of a cross with the front facing the rising sun, which symbolized the resurrection of Christ. Two immense towers flanked the front entrance of the cathedral, while the even taller bell tower stood proudly above the nave.

The churches built in that time had a dark side and a light side. Cemeteries and workshops were always built on the dark side, where the sun shone the least. Lychgates were usually erected to serve as a gateway near the cemetery to shield the coffin at a funeral from the elements until the clergy arrived. The light side of the church, on the other hand, always had anything associated with goodness built around that area. As if an omen, Crow and Muzzy entered through the dark side of the cathedral.

The cathedral office was in a secured section of the grounds. The door to the secured area had a window of reinforced glass with security wire mesh built into the pane. An office person who was walking down the hall saw the approach of the two apparent clergymen in their black cassocks through the small window and politely opened the secured door to let them in.

"Thank you," Crow said as he and Muzzy entered the hallway and the door shut behind them.

Instantly, the young man who had opened the door felt uneasy. He stepped aside and placed his hand on the doorknob of the nearest office as he smiled hesitantly at the two men. "Can I help you?"

"Ah, *oui*... I mean, yes," Crow said in a French accent, imitating an unknowing visitor to the cathedral. "Where is the vergers' office?"

"It is down that hall, second right then first left," the young man said as he pointed down the hallway. "You can't miss it. If there is no one there, the secretary can assist you."

"*Merci*," replied Muzzy in a deep voice like a clumsy fool.

The young man nodded as he opened the office door and slipped inside. The two imposters followed the office person's instructions and ended up at the office of the vergers. They opened the door and stepped inside, closing the door behind them. There was an administrative assistant there who assisted in the day-to-day office work for lay ministers, vergers, and other volunteer staff.

"We are here to speak with your head verger, please," Crow said politely.

"I'm dreadfully sorry, sir," the middle-aged woman said kindly. "He is already gone for the day. Perhaps, someone else could assist you. Phillips is our most senior staff member. Perhaps, he could offer his services."

Crow nodded approval. The office assistant swung her chair around to a scheduling book to try to discover where Phillips might be working.

"Ah, his schedule has him outside on the grounds behind the church. I would be happy to call him on his cell," she offered as she turned back to the two men.

Crow was already studying the layout of the cathedral and the church grounds on a map posted on the wall. The information on how to get to the crypt was not on the map. The map was a great piece of information for all the volunteers and guest clergy to use to get around in such a large area. However, at that moment, it did not serve his evil purpose. He was already thinking of how to ask where the crypt could be found. It was going to be difficult so as not to tip off their plans. He needed that information.

"That would be just fine," Crow said, his mind working quickly. "In fact, it was Mr. Phillips I was hoping to see."

"Oh, really?" the woman asked with a smile, thoroughly pleased with the turn of events. "Who shall I say is calling, sir?"

"Tell him it is a very old acquaintance of his who needs to complete a pilgrimage," Lark said slyly. "He's been expecting me. I was actually supposed to meet him in the crypt."

"Oh, in that case, you go ahead while I try his phone," the office assistant said cheerily. "When you leave, turn right. Go down that hallway, three doors on the left, and enter the stairs through the third door. The door is not marked, but the crypt in down the stairs. You can't miss it."

Believing that she was helping, she had accidently given away a verger secret of extreme importance and significance.

"This is my lucky day," Crow replied with a wicked smile.

And with that, the two imposters left the room and headed down the long hallway.

CHAPTER 40: TRAPPED

England, 2014

Phillips answered the cellphone only to be told he had guests coming down the stairs. A worried look overtook his face: he knew very well that he lived a quiet retired life in the background of the cathedral. For him to have guests coming to pay him a visit in the crypt, it was indeed an ill omen.

"We have some unwanted visitors coming down here," Phillips said as he ended the call and placed the phone in his pocket. "Quickly, help me close the door."

The group hurried across the room to the heavy door to push it closed so that they might hide in obscurity in the forgotten room. Michael and Steve were right behind Phillips as they reached the room's entrance and began to push the large iron and wood door.

Crow and his accomplice hurried down the corridors of the crypt. The crypt and its hallways were, indeed, a large maze. Crow quickly started to get confused as doubt clouded his sense of direction.

"This way…," an odd noise of cawing morphed into an old woman's voice whispered in Crow's mind.

He was puzzled at the voice, unsure of who the voice belonged to. He didn't challenge it and proceeded down a darker hallway. He then heard a commotion of footsteps and the pushing of something heavy as it scratched along the floor.

"Hurry! They are closing that heavy door there," whispered the voice.

Crow stopped and tapped Muzzy's arm. He pointed to the very old door being closed. With a surprise rush of speed, Muzzy charged and rammed his massive body into the doorway and kept the immense door from fully closing. Then with great strength, he forced the door open so that Crow could step in with his pistol already drawn.

Caesar was cawing excitedly that evil was upon them. His wings flapped, and his head turned at an angle.

"Step back!" Crow demanded.

Phillips, Michael, Steve, and Elizabeth all obeyed. Caesar became quiet and flew up into the rafters above the room before Crow and his associate could spot him. Muzzy, a former bouncer at a dive bar in Paris, entered the room as if a giant had entered a cave to intimidate all inside.

Crow quickly assessed the room.

"You!" Crow said, pointing at Michael with his gun. "You have the relic you showed me back at the other cathedral. You stole it from the trashcan. I know you have it! Give it to me!"

Phillips tried to speak. Crow turned his pistol towards the old man and cocked the gun.

"Shut up, whoever you are," Crow hissed. "I want that bone."

"Please," Elizabeth pleaded. "Please! We don't have it!"

Crow had begun to realize that things were going to get ugly, and he was going to have to kill everyone in the room. He began to survey the room's contents. He saw the maps, the stars, and even other bone fragments in glass boxes, and he began to calculate their worth to the guild and to his wallet.

"What is this place?" Crow asked, his eyes narrow and cruel.

"Michael, you were in the military and must be familiar with English naval history. Tell our friend—no, show him—what the phrase, 'We shall beat to quarters' means," Phillips said gently as he looked into Michael's eyes then glanced upwards over Crow's head.

There, perched upon two iron nails on the top of the door, was an old mace. It was a medieval weapon, but it was also used by vergers as a symbol of authority.

Suddenly, Caesar, who had been silently observing everything below, began to caw and flap his wings. The ruckus above them startled Crow and his lumbering associate.

At that instant, Michael jumped up and reached over Crow's head and grabbed the rusted iron mace. Crow's gun fired off a shot in protest. The bullet ricocheted off the stone wall behind them and narrowly missed Caesar as he flew out of harm's way. As Michael began to come back down, he crashed the mace into the skull of Crow, killing him instantly. Muzzy turned and dove onto the stone floor to catch his boss as he fell. The gun bounced to the floor where Steve picked it up and quickly pointed it at the fallen giant.

Caesar flew over to Elizabeth and landed on her arm. In the blink of an eye, the situation had changed them from being captives to victors.

Steve, with the gun pointed at Muzzy, glanced quickly to see if everyone was okay.

"Are we good?" asked Michael as he jerked the grisly mace from Crow's skull.

"Oh, my…," Phillips whispered in anguish as he began to fall to his knees in pain. A bright crimson wound on his chest was wet with his blood as that ricocheted bullet had finally met its terminal end.

"Phillips!" cried Michael, rushing to the old verger's side.

Michael dropped the mace and knelt down beside his new friend to hold him.

"You must see to it that these men are punished," Phillips said softly as he reached one hand into his pocket while the other pressed against the wound on his chest. "Alert the authorities as to what happened here. It's okay. My guild members will come here and make everything disappear."

"I will," Michael assured him. "Stay quiet, and we'll get help."

Phillips shook his head as he pulled the small box from his pocket. He reached up, and Michael held out his hand. Phillips placed the box in Michael's hand and pressed Michael's fingers closed around the relic.

"Remember your oaths. Serve…," Phillips whispered as he took his last breath.

Suddenly, Caesar went into a rage and flew about the room in anger. Elizabeth tried to catch him and calm him down, but he was not to have any part of it. His master had been slain by the henchmen.

"Enough of this nonsense!" screamed Muzzy as he grabbed the edge of the table with both hands to help himself stand up.

Steve pointed the pistol to reassure his prisoner that he was still in control and that he wasn't afraid to use the gun. The big man grinned, knowing the boy could probably only get one shot off before he reached him. Muzzy had taken worse in bar fights. He also knew if he could get that gun back, perhaps, his employers would pay him Crow's share as well as his fee when he gave them the bone.

Caesar, sensing the evil man's intensions, dove towards his face with claws outstretched to strike, and strike home they did. Caesar's claws found both of Muzzy's eyes wide open as his talons pierced into the eyes of the giant, blinding him. The man's reactions were too slow as both hands bore the weight of his body in an effort to pull himself to his feet using the table. He screamed in pain and then in fear, as he could no longer see.

The giant went into a blind rage as he stumbled to his feet. He swung his arms wildly as he swept back and forth trying catch Steve and the gun. Steve moved like an adept boxer in the ring, totally avoiding the large bear-like swings of his attacker.

Michael, putting on his backpack, picked up Phillips' keys from the floor where they had fallen in all the chaos.

"Come on!" he yelled as he ran to the door and beckoned for Elizabeth and Steve to come with him.

Elizabeth grabbed Caesar from the table upon which he had landed and headed for the door. In his confusion, Muzzy moved in the opposite direction as Steve, and Steve used it to his advantage to hurry to the door.

Michael, Steve, and Elizabeth, who had Caesar in her arms, scrambled out of the secret map room, pulling the heavy door behind them. Michael turned the iron key many different ways with multiple turns to scramble the door's special lock.

Everyone could hear the blinded man tearing up the room until he finally reached the mighty door and beat against it to no avail. The giant would be in there for a very long time. The Verger's Guild could reopen the door later and deal with its new, unruly occupant.

"Let's get out of here!" shouted Elizabeth as she turned with Caesar wrapped tightly in her arms and headed down the tunnel to where they had entered with her cousins following right behind her.

CHAPTER 41: THE TRAP IS SPRUNG

England, 2014

When the group emerged from the grassy entrance into the sunlight, they were instantly blinded by the brightness of the afternoon sun. Stunned, they stood quietly like three rabbits leaving their den.

Elizabeth suddenly found herself in a struggle with Caesar as he broke free from her arms to fly up to one of the cathedral's flying buttresses. Perched there like a dark gargoyle, he flapped his wings in protest and cawed three times, meaning "angry," "frustrated," or even "danger."

The three on the ground slowly got their vision back. There was a fresh breeze from the east, and it felt good for everybody to be out of the dark and dank tunnel.

"Well, well," a voice from behind Steven and Michael said. "Look what I found! I'll take that pistol now, if you please."

Steve froze still as he felt the owner of the mysterious voice press the barrel of a gun into his back. His eyes met Elizabeth's, as she stood opposite the two boys facing their attacker. He knew from the horror on Elizabeth's face who had spoken those words. Michael, familiar with the voice, had known instantly that it was Tommy's roommate, Bernard, and had turned halfway towards him before he had seen Vonyou's pistol aimed right at his brother. Slowly, Michael raised his arms in submission, and Elizabeth and Steve did the same.

"You three have been quite the sore spot for us," Bernard said calmly. He used the pistol to quickly point at the bulge in Michael's pocket. "I will take that finger bone now."

Michael knew that Bernard had them cold, and there was no mace above a doorway to help them escape their current predicament. He reached into his pocket and pulled out the ancient relic.

"Open it up so I can see it," Bernard demanded, eyeing the other two to make sure that no one was going to make a move.

Carefully, Michael opened the box and held it out to him. A sinister smile spread across Bernard's face.

"Excellent," Bernard whispered. He looked up at the gun still in Steve's hand that was raised over his head. "I'll take that gun now."

Bernard reached up and took Steve's gun and put it in his pocket.

From a tree in the garden behind the cathedral, a large ominous-looking crow flew over to the group and landed. The crow used its beak to place the stick it had been carrying in its mouth under a folded wing. It then cawed out as if in protest, and then, in the blink of an eye, the crow changed shape. The stick turned into a staff, and the crow turned into a disheveled old crone.

"I will take that bone," Cassandra said, holding her staff of magic towards Michael's outstretched hand.

Stunned, everyone paused and turned towards the old witch. Even Bernhard couldn't believe his eyes had seen the crow change into an old woman.

"Wait. You are Cassandra?" Bernard asked in amazement as he pushed his silver-rimmed glasses higher on his nose.

At that very moment, Michael lunged towards Bernard. The swiftness of Michael's actions stunned Bernard, and Bernard pulled the trigger as he was knocked to the ground, firing Vonyou's pistol and sending a bullet accidentally speeding towards Cassandra.

Cassandra, realizing that her final victory might be in danger of failing, flung her arm holding the staff faster than a hummingbird's wings in flight and cast a spell to freeze all time. Everything stood still. Even the bullet leaving the gun was frozen in midair.

Cassandra realized that her druid magic wouldn't last long enough for her to move out of the way, and she became frightened. If she cast the smoke spell, she could drift out of the way, but she wouldn't be able to hold her staff. Her beady black eyes quickly flashed back and forth as she gambled that when she changed form back into a crow instead, the bullet just might miss the smaller target. It was the lesser of two evils.

She waved her staff again and changed into her crow shape as time resumed with the changing of spells.

Her gamble almost worked. Her smaller size as a crow robbed the bullet of its target, but Cassandra's staff, the central focal point of all her strength and spells, was not so lucky. The wayward bullet smashed into the ancient stick of oak, shattering the miniature staff in two. The splinters flew wildly as the spells of Cassandra's magic floated away like dark, angry hornets leaving a nest. The staff was made useless.

The old crow cawed in horror as she suddenly realized that she was forever trapped in her crow body.

Dazed and confused, everyone quickly came to their senses and fought for the pistol that was still grasped in Bernard's hand. Michael had a good hold on it. Steve held down Bernard's shoulders, and Elizabeth picked up a large stone and clobbered Bernard over his forehead.

"Take that!" she said as she knocked him out, breaking his glasses.

Bernard collapsed like a sack of potatoes. The fight was over.

In the distance, police sirens wailed, telling the three that the authorities were on their way. They realized that someone must have heard the gunshot and commotion in the crypt and called the police to investigate the disturbance.

Michael and Steve stood up and walked over to Elizabeth. Even though they knew that there were going to be a lot of questions ahead, they were relieved that they had done their job and fulfilled their promise to protect the king's relics.

Suddenly, Michael remembered that he had let the box with the bone in it fall to the ground. He saw the empty box lying on the ground close to where he had stood earlier. He instantly knew that the bone must have fallen out of the box and into the grass in the confusion.

"Hey, help me find the bone, guys," Michael said, hurrying over to where the box had fallen. "I dropped it!"

Elizabeth and Steve quickly joined him, and the three looked around the grass as if they were children looking for an Easter egg.

As they searched for the bone, Cassandra quickly spotted the bone behind them. She walked over and picked up the bone with her beak and began to take flight. She was going to return to France and to the druid elders. There, perhaps, she could receive a special druid blessing to turn her back into a human.

Her wings began to take purchase of the air under her as she flapped to climb. Michael, hearing the sound of wings behind him, turned and made a brave attempt to catch her but failed as she slipped through his grasp.

"Come back, you blasted witch!" he screamed.

The images of Michael, Steve, and Elizabeth grew smaller and smaller beneath her until they practically vanished. Cassandra's little crow heart pumped as hard as it could as she climbed higher and higher. When she got about 300 feet up, she felt elated that she had the holy relic of Henry VIII's ring finger in her beak, clear skies ahead, the sun at her back, and nothing to stop her on the way to France.

CHAPTER 42: IN THE SHADOW OF THE CROW

England, 2014

Michael suddenly remembered the backpack he had been carrying and its contents. Quickly, he opened it up to expose his first and favorite drone, Wolfie. He took the drone out of its protective case, opened the drone's propellers, and turned it on. While he was doing this, Steve got out the drone's remote control and got it ready for his brother. Switching on the remote, Steve sent a command signal to the drone. The drone came to life with a quick pulse of rotation on each of the drone's four motors. Elizabeth helped too as she synced the visual monitor the Wolfie had with its forward-facing camera. Michael was then able to fly Wolfie as if he was the pilot.

The drone's motors began to hum like a hundred bees in unison. Michael held the drone up high with his right hand. He then nodded to Steve to bring Wolfie to full power to begin its chase of the witch. When Michael felt the drone pulling hard enough to escape his hand, he nodded to his brother and released the drone into the air.

Wolfie flew skyward like a hummingbird racing to the next flower for a sweet taste of nectar. Steve handed over the controller to Michael, and Elizabeth held up the monitor for him to use. The drone flew straight up towards Cassandra who was high in the sky. Michael intended to smash the drone into the black crow to make her drop the relic in her beak.

"Everybody keep an eye for where she might drop that bone when I hit her," Michael said as he pushed the drone to its maximum speed. "We can't lose her or the bone."

By then, Cassandra had climbed even higher and farther away from the cathedral grounds. It seemed to her as if nothing could stand in her way, but she was not aware of being pursued by Michael's drone. In less than half of a minute, she began to hear a buzzing sound. The sound was like the noise a new bumblebee makes when emerging from its little hole in the chewed wood that was its home during a cold winter: clumsy, noisy, and even loud as the bee's wings flap hard to achieve flight. The crow looked around with the bone in her mouth, but she couldn't see much or even anticipate what would happen next.

Suddenly, a fast-moving object flew by from underneath with incredible speed, making a loud buzzing swoosh as it passed her. She lost her balance, and the dangerous pass unnerved her to some degree. The drone continued straight for another 40 yards into the sun.

"Dammit! I missed her!" Michael said.

"Come on, Michael! Swing back around! Hurry!" shouted Elizabeth.

"No! Invert and then fall back on top of her!" advised Steve.

Michael knew what his brother was talking about. They had competed in a smash-and-grab tournament with several of their neighbors back in Georgia with their drones. The game's survivor got to keep the broken drone parts of all that were defeated. The flight tactic Steve wanted Michael to perform was the famous Immelmann Maneuver created by WWI German ace Baron von Richthofen, the Red Baron.

"I'm on it!" Michael said as he performed the tricky upside-down turn.

The drone did a complete flip and returned to take down its prey. That time, however, Cassandra was aware of her attacker, so she began a steep dive. With her wings drawn in, her body became a black dart that sped towards the ground with incredible speed. Michael's drone continued to pursue her.

"She going to lose us if she gets in those trees, Michael!" Elizabeth cried, anxiously bouncing on her heels.

As Cassandra approached the tree line, she swung out her wings to create an air brake which stopped her rapid descent. She flung the bone in her mouth skyward for a brief few seconds. As if in slow motion, Cassandra managed to pull off the impossible. By stopping in midair and spitting out the bone quickly, she managed to get out several magical caws that beckoned her followers to come to her aid.

Michael, not anticipating the crow's shrewd tactic, accidently let Wolfie pass harmlessly by her a second time.

"You missed her again!" Steve shouted. "Come on!"

Michael was getting frustrated. He was a skilled drone fighter, but the crow was making moves in the air that his machine couldn't match.

"I know, I know, Steven," Michael responded, using Steve's full name to show his irritation.

Within seconds, every crow from the forest below rose from the limbs and branches to flood the sky with their black wings, each crow screaming in reply that it would help. Like a massive black phalanx of winged soldiers, they rose to protect their druid master. Quickly, Cassandra snatched the bone back into her mouth and continued to fly towards France while her crow followers began their assault on Michael's drone. The sky grew black as even the sun couldn't penetrate the avian cloud.

Michael, Steve, and Elizabeth watched the monitor in disbelief as the black birds attacked the four-prop drone with alarming strength and numbers. Sharp black beaks and menacing claws scratched and pecked at Wolfie and its vital electronic organs. Suddenly, the monitor went dead as a claw pulled out the wire that connected the camera to the drone.

The three looked up as the birds broke the drone apart piece-by-piece as if Wolfie was in one of those smash battles for keeps back in the States. One prop broke from its housing after a crow sacrificed itself in the plastic blades; both prop and dead bird fell from the melee. Soon a second bird followed suit then a third.

"We're losing her, Michael," Steve said, shaking his head.

"She doesn't respond anymore to the remote," Michael replied.

"Oh, no! She's falling!" cried Elizabeth.

The three watched helplessly as Wolfie fell from the sky and smashed upon the ground, finally losing the life-and-death struggle in the air.

The phalanx of birds returned to their trees victorious, each crow shouting and crowing louder than the other that it was the bird that had killed the mechanical flying machine.

No one in the group next to the cathedral said a word as they watched Cassandra speed away to the east. The sound of approaching heavy footsteps and indistinct voices broke the silence behind them.

"It's the police, Michael," Steve said, as they all turned towards the sound. "They have found you. Do we run?"

"No, we stay. There's no use in running," Michael responded as he set the drone controller on the ground. He raised his hands in the air as Elizabeth laid down the monitor, and she and Steve raised their hands as well.

Three officers emerged over the crest of the ditch with their guns drawn. They looked down at Michael and the others.

"Stay where you are," commanded the brown-haired officer in the lead.

The three officers looked around them before descending slowly down into the ditch. They surveyed the scene quickly, noting the open door to the tunnel and Bernard laying on the ground.

"Protect, save, and serve," the lead officer said as he held up his right hand with a golden sigil ring.

Michael instantly recognized the ring, as it was the same verger's ring that David had worn on many occasions back at the army base in Afghanistan. He let out a sigh of relief and lowered his hands. "We all have sworn our oath, officer."

The officer nodded in approval, and Elizabeth and Steve lowered their hands, as well. Quickly, the police officers took over the crime scene. Any evidence of their presence there was taken into custody, including the gun and Bernard, who was still unconscious.

"There is a blinded bad guy in your secret vault. He is one of them," Elizabeth said as she pointed to Bernard."

"And Phillips was killed by the dead man in that same vault," added Steve.

Michael stepped forward. "They are part of the Bone Gatherers, officer. The two men in the vault also killed Mr. Lark, the verger from Chelmsford Cathedral. They were after the king's finger bone. My friend David's dying wish was for me to return it to that cathedral. I think they were also somehow responsible for the death of a young woman the other night outside a pub in London, as well as three people they mistook for my family at the Landmark Hotel."

"Thank you," the lead officer said, nodding his head. "You three have helped stop members of the secret society that has been a menace to our guild for ages. Phillips would be proud, if he were still alive."

"But we lost the finger bone," Michael said, frowning. "It's my fault that it's gone. It was carried away by a witch—I mean, crow. I tried to stop her, but I couldn't."

"We will find it again someday. This is what we do," the officer replied. "Our battle is never-ending. Devotion is a calling: we dearly love and follow for our king."

Michael nodded his head. "I understand now why my friend David's last words were about serving. It was part of who he was, and now it's part of who I am."

The officer smiled and then looked around the scene. "Within an hour, all of this will be gone. No one will ever know who these perpetrators were, for they will no longer exist. Phillips will be awarded posthumously for his gallantry. Funny, he always knew that this day might come, the day when one of us gives his life to a devotion that seemed just and right. We all have taken that vow."

An ambulance and a transport van for the three Americans arrived to return them to London. Thanks to the guild, a news flash would later be posted that Michael was not the man who had killed Lark or the others. While Michael finished out the remainder of his medical leave with Tommy, Elizabeth and Steve took their flight back to Atlanta and then traveled home.

CHAPTER 43: A DANCE WITH DEATH IN THE AIR

England, 2014

Cassandra, in her crow form, finally achieved sufficient altitude and set her course for France. She was satisfied that she had made a good escape.

Suddenly, the sun was no longer at her back. It was a strange feeling. As if a large cloud had moved in front of the sun, she found herself in a shadow. Then an immense object crashed down on top of her in midair. She could feel two old leathery talons digging into her feathered back. Thrown off-balance, she began to stall. The claws in her shoulders were unbearable and unrelenting. She tried to wiggle free by shifting her shoulders back and forth, but it was to no avail.

In her desperation, she thought that if she could summon up all of the strength she had left, perhaps she could cast a spell to rid her of the death hold she found herself in. Without her staff, however, she would have to let go of the bone in her beak to speak the spell.

The great bird that had Cassandra in his talons let forth several loud caws, speaking in the language that crows and ravens share. "It is I, Caesar, who has you now, Cassandra. You will not escape me!"

With his large black beak, he then began to peck violently on the back of Cassandra's head. Blood began to come out of each hole that his sharp beak inflicted.

Cassandra knew then that her past sins had come forward to be paid, but she would not allow her mission to be lost. If it took her last breath, she would curse every crow in the world to complete her objective and bring the fingerbone to her masters. Knowing she had only moments left, she painfully moved her left claw to grab hold of the bone so that she could speak, inflicting more pain and more blood loss as she exposed more of her neck and back to her attacker with the movement.

She stopped her attempts to fly or struggle free from Caesar's grasp. Burdened by the extra weight of the limp crow, Caesar faltered and had to cease his pecking to keep them both in the air, giving Cassandra the extra moments she needed to cast her spell.

Using every ounce of concentration, Cassandra reached deep within her, summoning all of the Druid magic that remained in her dying body. Her body began to tremble, and she opened her beak. As she did, wisps of greenish-grey smoke spewed forth from inside her and swirled around both her and Caesar. The mighty raven flapped his wings harder and moved higher and from side to side to escape the evil that spilled from Cassandra's beak.

As Caesar struggled, Cassandra continued to pull forth her dark magic. The greenish-grey tendrils of smoke grew darker, and the blackened vapor that poured from her open beak caught in the wind and was carried away, soon to spread to all corners of the Earth.

"Find the bone!" she whispered as the last wisp of magic seeped from her beak.

The ancient witch then passed away. Her lifeless body released the finger bone from her claw. Like a winged seed, it fluttered around and around until it landed in the grassy plain below.

Caesar released his lethal grip on Cassandra's lifeless body, letting it fall heavily to the ground. The grand raven, realizing he had let the old witch drop his master's bone by accident, then raced towards the ground to rescue the finger bone before her magic could summon hundreds of crows. He knew that the first bird to find the bone would be the ruler of all the crows. Driven by Cassandra's curse, each crow would hunt for the bone relentlessly, and he had to beat them to it.

Caesar landed safely in the field below, but he was taken aback. It was too late, for already in the field were hundreds of crows and even some wild ravens. Every one of them had their beak into the ground or grass. Hunting and pecking, the throng of Cassandra's followers had started their search. More arrived each minute as her spell was carried by the wind throughout the forest and the lands beyond.

Caesar tried desperately to look as well, but he was constantly under attack by his smaller cousins who despised his large raven presence. Some of the crows took flight, and Caesar looked up to each bird to see if it had found the bone. Other crows grabbed small sticks and, in doing so, thought they had found the royal treasure. The crows would then fly up to the nearest branch and proclaim that they were the new ruler but then find out that it was false. Driven to madness by the curse, the crows even began to attack each other, stealing from a fellow crow if it had a stick or a piece of straw that looked even remotely like a finger bone.

Caesar then, at last, spied one crow in the throng. That bird had something different than a stick or piece of straw, for it was, indeed, the bone of his master. The crow flew to the nearest tree and announced its victory. It then opened its wings and mounted to the sky, headed towards France.

Caesar quickly moved to get clear of the birds around him. He began to flap his wings to escape upwards. Sensing that the large raven was going to attack their new leader, the mass of crows grew infuriated. They moved like a massive black curtain to block their raven captive from any attempt to pursue their ruler. Each time Caesar tried to give chase, a new wave of crows would beset him, pummeling him with their wings and clawing at him with their sharp talons.

Again and again, Caesar tried to escape to rescue his master's bone, but the crows were too much for him. He fell to the ground, wounded and bleeding, as he watched the crow with the bone it its beak fly into the distance. Seeing the mighty raven was wounded and could not follow them, the rampaging crows took flight, following their new ruler and the bone.

Caesar watched helplessly as the cloud of black birds faded into the distance, knowing that the battle that he had fought for five hundred years had just taken a new turn. It was not the end, only a new beginning.

EPILOGUE

The new ruler of the crows never made it to France. It was not Caesar who stopped it, but the other crows. As Cassandra's spell reached every corner of the Earth, its sole purpose of finding the bone overtook the mind of every crow. The greed and power struggle that plagued man from the beginning of time worked in the hearts of the crows, as well. One by one, the ruler would be killed, only to have another take its place. The goal of returning the bone to the Druid masters became secondary to the crows' desire to rule, and the bone was taken further and further away from France.

Caesar recovered from his injuries and continued his quest to recover his master's finger bone. He followed it throughout Europe and into Africa, stopping at the Anglican churches along the way to gather news from any vergers that might be there. At All Saints Cathedral in Cairo with its circle of raven-feather-like arches shooting skyward, its architecture forming a unique crown, the mighty raven discovered that the bone had been seen. It had been spotted in the mouth of a crow aboard a cargo ship leaving for the Americas by a pilgrimage of vergers making their way from Egypt to Israel. Caesar then stowed away on a steamer and crossed the ocean, making his way to the United States.

In the late summer of 2017, Caesar spotted the bird with the bone at long last. He chased it for several weeks before losing its trail in Gainesville, Georgia, where the Cotter family resided. At that time, Hurricane Irma swept through the Atlantic Ocean. Man and beast felt the wrath of nature's fury. Extreme wind and rain pummeled all below and in the trees. The crow who had the bone at that time was also still in Georgia. It was killed by lightning when the bolt hit the tree branch that the crow was perched on. The bone fell into the wind, which carried it aloft and into obscurity.

The crow followers tried in vain to fly against the wind and storm to retrieve their prize. They searched and searched for their beloved artifact, but they never found it. Their desperate search continues to this day, as does Caesar's.

So, as this tale draws to a close, know this, my good friend: Cassandra's curse will course through the veins of every crow until it finds that one true prize. And as you, too, have now become keepers of the vergers' secret, I ask you to keep watch. Whenever you should see a crow hunting and pecking in the grass of some field, yard, or glen, remember that bird is searching for one thing, and one thing only: the finger bone of Henry VIII. If you should spot it, snatch it away before it is lost again. For just as the crows' and Caesar's search continues, so does the quest of the Verger's Guild.

YOU MAY ALSO ENJOY

Wolf on the Lake by Ed Thilenius

Wolf on the Lake is the first book in the Cotter family trilogy where Michael, Steve, and Elizabeth discover a terrorist plot in their own backyard. Available for purchase online. Find out more at: edthilenius.com.